AF123457

The Baker's Touch

The Baker's Touch

VIBE a Steamy Romance Series #1

Lynn Chantale

4 Horsemen Publications, Inc.

The Baker's Touch
Copyright © 2021-2024 Lynn Chantale. All rights reserved.
Published By: 4 Horsemen Publications, Inc.

4 Horsemen
Publications, Inc.

4 Horsemen Publications, Inc.
PO Box 417
Sylva, NC 28779
4horsemenpublications.com
info@4horsemenpublications.com

Cover & Illustration by Connor Bryan
Typesetting by Valerie Willis

All rights to the work within are reserved to the author and publisher. No part of this publication may be reproduced, stored in a retrieval system, or transmitted in any form or by any means, electronic, mechanical, photocopying, recording, scanning, or otherwise, except as permitted under Section 107 or 108 of the 1976 International Copyright Act, without prior written permission except in brief quotations embodied in critical articles and reviews. Please contact either the Publisher or Author to gain permission.

All characters, organizations, and events portrayed in this novel are either products of the author's imagination or are used fictitiously.

All brands, quotes, and cited work respectfully belongs to the original rights holders and bear no affiliation to the authors or publisher.

Library of Congress Control Number: 2021942122

Paperback ISBN-13: 978-1-64450-301-0
Audiobook ISBN-13: 978-1-64450-512-0
Ebook ISBN-13: 978-1-64450-300-3

Table of Contents

ACKNOWLEDGMENTS IX
CHAPTER ONE 1
CHAPTER TWO 21
CHAPTER THREE 34
CHAPTER FOUR 59
CHAPTER FIVE 78
CHAPTER SIX 96
CHAPTER SEVEN 106
AUTHOR BIO 111

Dedication

This book is respectfully and lovingly dedicated to anyone who knows what it is to overcome and succeed when life strives to keep you down. Here's to getting back up and being stronger for the test.

Acknowledgments

To my editor for your advice and compassion. Thank you for having an open mind. I'd also like to thank the members of the SWFCB for all of their resources and for being a support for those with blindness and visual impairments. You are a continual inspiration. Also, to my dad for the countless phone calls to clarify a detail.

As always, I thank God for the talent and creativity He's given me.

Chapter One

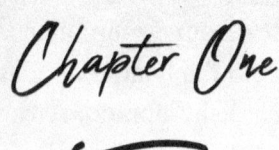

A small throng of people gathered in the wide tiled foyer. The distant chatter of conversation mingled with soft music and the occasional burst of laughter.

Mr. VIP eyed the small group of people with some hostility. *Look at them. So successful and happy at this New Year's Eve gathering. How dare they be happy when I am struggling.* He clenched his hands at the thought.

Didn't they know his world was falling apart? Didn't they know he was suffering? Or were they too wrapped up in their own relationships and businesses to notice he had withdrawn more than usual?

They were supposed to be his friends, his colleagues, his support system.

And not *one* of them noticed.

No. Not when he had stopped bringing his wife around. Nor when he no longer hosted any social gatherings at his home. They hadn't even noticed he no longer discussed his business, his passion.

They hadn't noticed *anything*.

Breathing deep, allowing the rising anger to swell and dissipate enough, he unclenched his hands and exhaled. Once more, he was the calm collected man they all knew him to be.

"Has the rest of our group arrived?" said Abigail Anderson. She held the handle of a large, attentive but aging, yellow, English Labrador retriever named Percy.

"I think we're still waiting on Penelope."

"Let me grab a quick picture before we move," Geneva Martin said. She walked a few steps away, her heels clicking on the polished floor. "I can't believe I'm getting a chance to be here," Geneva gushed. "My mom always described the lobby as classy. You know, lots of marble and crystal chandeliers." Her words snapped out in a feminine voice as she rapidly instructed the person with the camera to tilt the cameral left, then right. The soft click of a shutter snapping followed, echoing off the high ceilings. "I can't wait to post these on my website."

Mr. VIP edged out of the frame. It wouldn't do for Geneva to capture his image just yet. At least, not right now. He didn't want to be on her website. And he still couldn't understand how she made any money reviewing products, posting pictures, and participating in interviews.

He had to admit ... she had quite the following. Not only with the sighted, but those with any form of blindness. No matter how he felt about the others, he grudgingly gave Geneva his respect.

She wasn't like the others who were involved in mixed relationships—a sighted person partnered with a blind person. Like he used to be. No. She had the good sense to marry another visually disabled person.

Mr. VIP surveyed the people in the lobby. None of them sported an afro. The hair was the only identifier he had for Geneva's husband. If he didn't see him, Geneva must be here alone tonight. She raised her phone again, and he shifted out of range, putting a stucco column and large potted plant between them.

She reminded him of his daughter, whom he wasn't allowed to see because of his *ex*. His ex thought him incompetent because of his failing vision. She didn't feel that was a problem when she was taking his money, he thought with some bitterness. Those thoughts only re-kindled his anger. And that was another thing he no longer liked about this group. They didn't act like a bunch of blind people. Blind people were supposed to be helpless and catered to, not going around snapping pictures and running businesses.

Mr. VIP removed his glasses. What had been clear and in focus a moment ago was now blurred and unrecognizable. He polished the thick lenses on a square of cotton before returning them to his face. Once again, he could see, but not like he used to. Without his glasses, people and objects were just little fuzzy blobs of color. At least with the correction, shapes were more discernible, and if he stayed within a ten-foot distance of what he was viewing, his vision was like everyone else's. Beyond those limits, he was happy just to identify color.

"I think I hear Penelope," Time announced.

Mr. VIP turned and spotted the speaker, Time—an older black man with a shock of silver hair—and allowed his gaze to linger. The matching beard and mustache made it impossible to guess the man's age. He'd heard Time was a semi-pro wrestler but didn't put much stock into it. There was no way a man as old as Time could wrestle.

A soft chuckle drew his attention to the entry way. If he moved a little closer…

The woman ran a bakery; how in the world did she draw so many people? Someone was already helping her from her coat while another gushed. He moved beside the column he'd used for shelter a moment ago. And now she was hugging her adoring fans.

"Great!" Geneva stated. "Now, we can get a picture with everyone."

Mr. VIP nearly snorted aloud. Had Geneva really waited for *Penelope*? They wouldn't have waited for him if the roles had been reversed. And Penelope was the worst of them.

A flash of vibrant blue caught his peripheral, and he turned to look. *There she is … with her white cane, wide smile, and pretty face.* He moved to keep her in sight. She was so independent and worked in her family's bakery. If that wasn't enough for him to despise her, she also had a successful boyfriend. All the things he no longer had. It wouldn't take much to get rid of these people. *They will never see it coming.*

He swallowed his rising laughter at the joke. He could walk up to any of them right now and…

Penelope Bishop accepted a hug from one of her regular customers. "Thank you so much for volunteering tonight, Patsy. This means the world to me."

Patsy patted her hand. "Darling, you inspire me. Every time I try to have a pity party, I think of you and your can-do attitude."

Heat flooded her cheeks. "If only you knew what it takes to keep that attitude," she downplayed the compliment.

Patsy laughed. "I can only imagine. Now go on. Your friends are waiting for you." Her footsteps faded on the marble.

Penelope tuned into the bubble of voices, the rich baritone of Time, Geneva's lilting alto with its slight lisp, Rodney's quiet tones which always reminded her of a timid professor. Then there was Amelia's cultured voice and Abigail's distinctive, but faint New Yorker accent.

"It sounds like the gang's all here," Penelope sang out. She was glad to be amongst her friends again.

"We were just about to take a picture," a man with a deep rumbling voice announced.

"Ah, Geneva must be here with her camera." Penelope grinned. "It's so good to *see* everybody."

"I am," Geneva confirmed. "Abigail, Amelia, Rodney, and Time are here too."

The group shuffled as Penelope accepted hugs and well-wishes.

Penelope was a little overwhelmed with the exuberant greetings and was grateful for the reprieve when Abigail pulled her aside.

"We really need to do lunch," Abigail murmured into Penelope's ear.

"Stop by the bakery some time," Penelope said as she briefly held the other woman's hand. "Is everything all right? The bar?"

Abigail was the proud owner and operator of a popular bar and eatery. "We'll talk later," Abigail promised. "It's too much to go into now."

She held to Abigail's hand when she would've pulled away. "You're sure everything is fine? Nothing wrong with the family or grandkids?" Penelope probed. She knew the relationship between Abigail and her children was tenuous at best. The saving grace was the grandkids. The adults could be civil around the children. If you need to talk now, we can find a quiet corner."

Abigail squeezed her hand. "You are such a good friend. Nothing so dramatic. It will keep for another day."

Penelope smiled in the general direction of her friend. "Sounds good. Are we ready to go in?"

They formed a processional of sorts, the blind leading the blind as they entered the ballroom proper. Here, they were engulfed in activity but not overwhelmed.

The group parted ways and Penelope found herself alone in the crowd. For a moment, she listened, absorbing the ebb and flow of the room. She caught what she thought was a snippet of Sam's voice and turned in that direction.

"There you are!"

"I was just making my way to you," Penelope stated. "Sounds like a good crowd."

"I suppose," Sam grunted. He grabbed her hand and tugged her across the crowded floor.

Penelope stumbled as she followed along, mumbling apologies when she bumped into someone or something. "Slow down," she admonished.

He ignored her request. "There's someone I want to speak with before they leave."

When Sam paused, hoping to catch sight of the person he wanted to speak with, Penelope tuned into the surrounding conversations.

As unobtrusively as possible, she released his hand, then gripped his elbow instead. Holding him this way allowed her better maneuverability while anticipating his stops and starts.

"…demolished. There are some stubborn owners in that part of the city." Penelope paused at the snippet of conversation and strained her ears to hear more.

"It's a high traffic part of town. What did you expect them to say? Yes to your proposal?" someone said with disdain. "They're old farts who don't know when to sell."

"They're family-owned businesses that have been there forever. They'll soon see the error of refusing."

At the hard tug on her bicep, she stumbled forward as she was pulled along, the rest of the conversation lost in the laughter swirling around the room. Music mingled with easy chatter, and she could just make out the rhythmic stride of dancing. Sam, her date and companion for the last four months, would rather hold idle conversations than ask her to dance.

At his abrupt stop, she bumped into Sam's shoulder; the soft wool of his suit brushed her nose. Penelope sniffed. A familiar blend, sweet like jasmine and nutmeg tickled her nostrils. She frowned, leaning closer to Sam. The scent blended with his spicy aftershave, along with a tang of something ... earthier.

"Did you need something?"

"No, Sam," Penelope said as she shifted beside him.

"All right." None too gently, he shook off her hand and turned away. "Bill, did you receive the proposal I sent over yet? I tell you, there is major money to be made in this endeavor."

From the direction of his voice, he had his back toward her and was gradually moving away. She huffed and patted her evening bag, making sure her cane was still inside. He had a habit of removing it when they were together, and she wanted to make sure he hadn't done the same tonight.

Although, if he had, she was familiar with the ballroom, and there were enough volunteers to assist her if needed. While sponsored by several large companies, one of which Sam worked for, the proceeds of tonight's gala were all benefiting The Commission for the Blind, a nonprofit organization that helped visually impaired individuals gain the education and skills needed to live a full and productive life.

And it was near and dear to her heart. The agency had helped her retain her independence.

Retinitis pigmentosa, a degenerative eye disease attacking the retina, had robbed her of her sight by the time she'd reached fifteen, a permanent factor in her life. Part of her was relieved to be no longer living in that limbo of seeing some things while completely missing others. But then, she had to deal with people like Sam. A man who was supposed to like her for who she was, but lately he'd left her feeling cold and alone. *Will I ever find true love?*

All week Sam had grumbled about escorting her to the event, but a few days ago he'd switched his tune, even going the extra mile and hiring a limo for the evening. Her instinct had warned her that the sudden change of heart had nothing to do with her. So why did he really want to be here tonight?

She tilted her head, listening for Sam's braying tenor. He was still droning on about business or whatnot.

"You look quite amazing this evening," sin and smoke purred near her left shoulder.

She pivoted in that direction, not quite catching the voice. "Thank you."

Warm fingers trailed down her bare arm, gripping her hand. A sizzle sped through every nerve of her body. It wasn't just his touch but also his nearness. She was used to people's closeness, but this man's nearness was unnerving. Almost possessive. Each time she inhaled, her breasts touched his jacket.

"Would you care to dance?"

He was so close, his lips grazed the delicate shell of her ear, sending tingles down her spine and straight to her nipples.

A smile creased her lips. "I'm sorry. Do I know you?" she asked, not recognizing the speaker.

"In time, you will."

Penelope tilted her head. The dulcet tones were scintillating, but between his low volume and the loud background noise of the room, she still couldn't identify him. "I'm blind. Your voice sounds familiar, but I can't quite place it."

"I know. It's all good. I've been admiring you from across the room, and I noticed your date seems to have deserted you for the moment."

She bit her lip, not quite sure how to process this information. "He found one of his buddies to discuss business."

"His loss. If I had such a beautiful woman as my date, I wouldn't let you out of my sight for anything."

Pleasure stole through her at the compliment. "Thank you."

"Would you like to dance?"

"I'd love to."

He tucked her hand through the crook of his arm, and they moved forward. "Your dress is stunning."

Heat flushed her cheeks, delighted that her mystery man had actually noticed, while her date had not. Though her mother had described it to her in great detail over the phone, Penelope could only imagine the sequins and rhinestones dripping from the halter-style evening gown. Sam hadn't bothered to give her a compliment. He'd only said her lipstick was smeared.

Her heels clicked over a wooden surface. Vibrations traveled from the floor through the soles of her shoes toward the rest of her body. Her companion paused long enough to sweep her into his arms.

She stiffened. It shouldn't matter that she didn't know this stranger. All he wanted was a dance, nothing more. But being in his embrace, even for this dance, stirred a desire in her veins.

"Something wrong?"

"N-*no*."

He splayed his fingers against her back and swayed to the music. "Relax. Just one dance."

Relax. That was easy for him to say; he wasn't the one feeling a bit turned on at the moment. She slowly exhaled and allowed the tension to seep from her limbs.

He drew her closer, not too much, but enough to feel his body heat and the soft scrape of his suit jacket against her skin.

She wanted to press closer; dancing with this man felt like the most natural thing in the world, unlike with Sam where she constantly had to stay alert for shuffling feet. This man kept her close, leading her around the floor as if they had danced together for their entire lives.

"You're very graceful," he murmured, holding her a little tighter as a breeze ruffled her hair.

Another couple brushed by them.

"I feel safe with you," she blurted, then clamped her lips shut. She shouldn't have said that, but it was the truth. No one had ever put her at ease in such a short amount of time. Relying on her fellow man was a daily thing, especially when she misstepped or walked into the wrong store. But this man had an air about him that put her at ease, even if he didn't want to give his name.

"Who taught you how to dance?" He maneuvered her around the floor. Music and the murmur of voices grew quieter. *We must be farther away from the dancers and speakers.*

"My father. He was a dance champion for many years, which is how he met my mom, though she never danced professionally. He taught me as a way to trust my instincts as well as my partner."

"He did an excellent job."

She inclined her head, her hair sliding over one shoulder. "Who taught you how to dance?"

"An after-school program when I was a teen. It just stuck." His hand slid a little lower on her back. "I'm really glad I kept with it."

"I am too."

Left turn. His thigh brushed hers, and his hand slipped to the curve of her hip. Three short steps and a right turn. She held her breath as his fingers grazed the swell of her derriere, then returned to her hip. The contact was brief, but enough to jumpstart her libido. Lust dampened her panties and tightened her nipples. All from a simple waltz around the floor?

She had Sam in her life, but he never made her blood heat and she never really felt safe in his arms either. She stopped dancing.

"Is something the matter?"

"I-I think I should go powder my nose."

His throaty chuckle reached her ears. "Sure thing." He threaded her hand through the crook of his arm. "Looks like a lot more people have arrived since we started dancing. Stick close."

She nodded and swallowed. Sam would never have told her anything like that. He'd have just dragged her through the crowd with no warning. Maybe it was time to let him go.

Her best friends, Moira and Violet, would be thrilled if she kicked Sam to the curb. They never liked him. They obviously saw something in him that she wasn't aware of… well, more like in denial about, until now. *Maybe it is time to make a clean break.*

She stumbled into her nameless dance partner when someone jostled her from behind. He curved an arm around her shoulder, steadying her.

"Are you okay?"

She chuckled. "Yeah."

"We're almost to a clear spot, and then you can use your cane."

"You're not freaked out about me using a mobility device?" She tried to keep the defensive note from her voice but failed.

"Are you kidding? That thing is like Moses' staff. It can part a crowd of people at two paces." Humor filled his statement. "You can use that thing as often as you like."

Her shoulders sagged in relief. How much had she changed to garner Sam's approval? And when had it mattered that she fit in to his perfect world? After tonight, *no more*. If he couldn't accept her for who she was, then he didn't deserve to be in her life.

Their footsteps were muffled on the thick commercial carpeting, then clicked across linoleum. She pulled a small scope-like item from her purse. A flick of her wrist, and it flared into a cane, the quiet snap assuring her it had locked into place.

"I see you have a new cane."

"This one fits in my purse." How long had this man been watching her?

He lifted her hand and placed it on a smooth surface. "I'll wait here, and then return you to your date for the evening."

She nodded and pushed open the door. If memory served correct, the sinks were to her left while the bathroom stalls were five steps to the right, just around another corner.

She turned left. Between the cane and trailing her fingers along the slightly rough wall, she found an open sink. All she needed was a moment to compose herself. *I wonder if my friends had arranged for this mystery man to find me. And if so, I am not sure if I should thank them or yell at them.* Either way, she got the impression that she knew this person.

A smile curved her lips. She liked the idea of not knowing his identity, but she wished he'd at least give her his name.

The door swooshed open behind her, and giggling echoed off the walls. Penelope slid her hands along the cool metal surface until water sluiced into the bowl. *Ah, motion sensors.* She smiled. *Even better.* She quickly washed and dried her hands.

At the sweet floral scent she snapped up her head. It was a very distinctive perfume, one that had been following her all night. A couple of doors slammed shut, followed by several lock clicks.

"So you two actually had sex in one of the offices?"

"It was amazing," the other woman said, a hint of regret shadowing her somewhat cultured voice. "I feel bad though. His girlfriend is here tonight, and she has no idea what's been going on."

"You mean you're the other woman?" Awe and a bit of mirth filled the companion's voice.

"He says the relationship is flat, and well, he doesn't want to hurt her feelings because she's blind."

Penelope sucked in a gasp, her heart pounding. *Of all the things...* She blinked away the tears burning her eyes. *Don't cry over that man.* Smoothing a hand down the front of her dress, she carefully made her way toward the door. If she hadn't made up her mind before, she was certain now. She and Sam were done.

"Have you met the girlfriend?"

Penelope strained to hear the answer even as she trailed her fingers along the wall.

"No, but I've seen her around. She can even dance." Is that envy she detected? "Anyway, she's got this mane of gorgeous red hair, and a dress I'd kill to have."

Swallowing hard, Penelope yanked open the door, misjudged the distance and smacked her head on the edge.

A hand clamped over her wrist and pulled her into the hall. "Are you okay?" Gentle hands cradled her face, brushing her hair aside.

"Just peachy." She tried to squirm away from his inspection, but he held her still. "You really don't have to do that."

"You're not bleeding, but there's a nice little knot forming. You should really get some ice on it." He smoothed her hair back into place. "What was your hurry?"

She turned away. "I needed to get out of there."

He caressed her cheek. "I can see you, Penelope. You have tears on your lashes, and you're not smiling anymore." Heat from his body enveloped her as he moved closer. "What happened?"

Laughter spilled from the bathroom, and she stiffened. She felt him shift, his jacket brushing her arm.

"Are they pretty?"

"I guess, if a man likes the starving model look." His warm breath fluttered a curl on her face. "Did they say something to you?"

"One of them is sleeping with Sam," she muttered.

A sharp intake of breath followed. She inclined her head and stepped forward. It wouldn't be difficult to find her way out of the hotel. Hell, it was New Year's Eve, and there were a fleet of taxis lined up to take partygoers home. She could hail one of those.

A firm hand on her shoulder halted her forward momentum. "Then you're better off without him."

"Yeah. Thanks." She shook off his hand and continued walking. There were forty steps between where she stood and the ballroom. Finding Sam and smacking him across the shins would be another matter.

"What are you doing?"

"Going to give that cheating bastard a piece of my mind and then … have a glass of champagne."

"There you are," Sam said as soon as she stepped into the busy ballroom.

"You actually noticed I was gone?"

"There's someone I'd like to introduce you to." Sam all but pulled her away from her mystery man, then folded her cane. "You don't need this here." Contempt oozed from his voice.

Penelope dug in her heels. She wasn't going to let him drag her all over a crowded ballroom. "Actually, I do. I'm sure if you look around, you'll find others with similar visual aids. I believe there are a few service animals here as well."

"But they are not with me. I had no idea there were so many broken people in the world." He jerked her forward, and she stumbled to keep up. "There is someone I need you to meet, then you can return and mingle with your kind."

"My kind?" She was too taken aback by his statement to do more than sputter. A soft floral scent drifted to her nostrils, and she stiffened.

"Penny, I'd like you to meet Sheila. My company just hired her as one of its researchers."

"Sam is being modest," Sheila said. "I've been staring at your dress all evening. It is to die for."

Penelope bit the inside of her cheek and plastered what she hoped was a genial smile on her face. "That's a lovely fragrance you're wearing, Sheila. Jasmine, isn't it?"

A startled gasp reached her ears, and Sam shifted beside her.

"Why, yes. How did you know, Penny?"

"Penelope."

"Penelope," Sheila repeated.

"It's a very distinctive fragrance, and one I've smelled on more than one occasion."

Sam cleared his throat. "Penny…"

"Just because I'm blind doesn't mean the rest of my senses don't work. If you wanted out of the relationship, all you had to do was say so. I didn't need to overhear the exploits of my boyfriend broadcasted in the ladies' room." She stared in Sam's general direction. *I'd love to see the expression on his face right now.* Instead, she listened to him swallow and tug at his clothes.

"Really, Penny, you're imagining things."

She jerked away from him. "Sheila's perfume is all over your clothes, Sam. Now I know why you wanted to be here this evening, and I'm glad it had nothing to do with me." Penelope spun on her heel, stepped forward and met a solid wall of muscle.

She heard her name called along with a protest. Both of which were lost in a swirl of clothing, voices, and music. A strong arm encircled her shoulders, drawing her farther into the crowd.

Heat burned her cheeks. On top of everything else, she couldn't even storm out of the ball room without running into someone.

"Ready for that champagne?" her mystery man whispered into her ear once they stopped moving.

She swallowed. "You saw everything?"

He lifted her hand and placed her palm on his cheek. His head bobbed up and down, but there was more. His jaw was tight, and a corner of his mouth drooped. *Is he upset on her behalf?* The thought pricked her feminine pride, but at the same time, he had witnessed her humiliation.

She lowered her head.

"No, don't do that. Keep your head up." He placed a hand at her waist. "Besides, both of them stood there mortified at your declaration. The woman even slapped him and ran off through the crowd. He didn't look too pleased at the turn of events."

Excitement buzzed around them, and cheers rose. The crowd began counting down.

"He is absolutely not worth your time, and he didn't appreciate you."

A tear slipped beneath her lashes.

"I want you to know one thing, Penelope."

"Not fair. I don't even know your name."

He hooked an arm around her waist and drew her against his solid frame. "All you need to know is this." And as the crowd screamed "one" his mouth met hers.

She stood frozen, lost in a kiss that melted her soul, stirred her desire, and mended her heart. He coaxed her lips apart, his tongue darting along the seam. She curled her fingers in the lapels of his jacket as she opened for him, their tongues dueled for supremacy until she finally submitted.

Time stood still, the chorus of voices singing Auld Lang Syne faded as he clutched her tighter. His mouth never stopped moving on hers, becoming the very air she breathed. To stay in this stranger's embrace would be just what she needed, but a dance and a kiss did not make a relationship. Still, she wanted the passion and acceptance he offered.

"Happy New Year," he muttered against her lips.

"Same to you. What's your name?"

He kissed her again. "I'm sorry. I have to go."

Before she could protest, she was alone in the crowd. She touched her lips. If she didn't do anything else this year, she would at least find out who she had just kissed.

Chapter Two

Penelope allowed her head to fall forward as softness swept her skin in a caress. Each deliberate stroke sent a trickle of desire down her thighs. She squeezed her legs together, hoping to relieve the building ache. The small movement earned her a sharp slap on her bare behind. She bit back a gasp as pleasure and pain rolled through her.

"Be still." His whispered command left her wanton, while his warm breath tickled her ear. He soothed away the sting with the palm of his hand, and she fought her body's urge to press against him. "Tell me what you want."

She bit her lip as he rubbed his chest against her back. The cotton of his shirt scraped across her sensitized flesh. One hand drifted up, over her ribcage to cup her breast. The other went south and dipped a skillful finger into her damp heat. Her head fell against his shoulder. She widened her stance to give him better access. He lingered for a moment, rolling her nipple between his index finger and thumb, plunging a finger in and out of her slick heat, and his lips grazed the spot just below her ear.

A whimper left her lips.

"My beautiful Penelope, you are so sexy to me," he murmured against her skin. The flick of his tongue sent more delicious tingles racing down her spine. She tugged on the fur-lined cuffs binding her wrists above her head.

Abruptly, he stepped away.

She tensed, her heart skipping a beat as she realized she'd moved.

"You're learning."

She could hear the smile in his voice. He brought his hand down on the rounded portion of her behind. The momentary sting rolled into pleasure. He spanked her, each smack a little harder than the one before.

A gasp escaped as her butt warmed. She wanted more. Relished the bit of pain with passion. He pressed his front to her back and cupped her breasts. His erection wedged between the crack of her behind, while the coarse material of his slacks rubbed her tender cheeks just right. She couldn't stop from curving into the heat of his body.

"Please." She needed release, needed to feel his hands everywhere, bringing her to ecstasy and beyond.

He palmed her mons before plunging two fingers into her heat. "Is that what you want?"

She moved against his hand, a moan stuck in the back of her throat. "Yes."

He tapped her clit with his thumb. "Or more of this?"

Pleasure rippled through her veins and pulsed between her legs. "Yes."

Slowly, he thrust in and out, while he teased her nipple. His mouth found hers, his lips cool and commanding as they coaxed hers apart. Their tongues dueled, fighting for dominance. He released her breast to let his hand drift up her torso and rest at her throat.

Muffled ringing filtered through the silence. No. Now was not the time for interruptions. Already, his touch was fading.

The shrill noise grew louder.

"Damn!" Penelope sat upright, snatching the intrusive object from her nightstand. "This better be good."

It never failed. The same dream.

For the last few weeks, ever since that New Year's Eve kiss, she'd had the same vivid sex dream. Whenever she got to the good part with her dream lover, she was always interrupted before she climaxed. Even now, her body hummed for release.

"This is your security company. An alarm has been triggered at your place of business. Would you like me to dispatch the police?" the calm, efficient voice purred in her ear.

Her shop? "Yes. Do that and I'll meet them there. Thank you." She kicked the covers off, the erotic dream momentarily forgotten. Penelope fumbled for the clock, her fingers finding the button.

"2:47AM," the mechanical voice blurted.

"Ugh." She pushed to her feet.

This was not how she wanted to spend her morning. First her sex dream with the mystery man from New Year's Eve, and now, her shop. She moved to the phone, felt for the tiny raised bumps and pushed one.

The phone on the other end rang several times before it was answered. "Did you mean to call me this early, Miss Penelope?" the gravelly voice on the other end mumbled.

"Yes, James, I did. I'm sorry to wake you, but the alarm went off in the shop. I need to be there."

"I'll be out front in ten minutes." He sounded more alert now.

"Thank you." She hung up the phone.

With her head held high, she slowly made her way from her bedroom down the hall to the bathroom. Showered and dressed, she met James on the front porch. Early morning cold permeated her still damp hair. She shivered as she struggled into her coat.

"Miss Penelope, you'll catch your death walking out here in this cold night with wet hair and no coat on." James grabbed the collar of her heavy jacket and draped it over her shoulders. "Has Mrs. Tilman seen you?" He sighed. "Probably not if you're out here like this."

She stifled a chuckle. "I didn't want to wake her for this. I left her a message explaining there was an emergency at the shop." Salt crunched beneath her booted feet as she allowed James to lead her down the slippery walk. She misstepped on a slick spot and would've fallen if not for the gentleman's strong grip.

"Careful."

"Yeah," she agreed.

Once inside the vehicle, she breathed a sigh of relief. It was just too damn cold in the middle of February. Winters in Michigan were the worst for early morning bakery hours. The shop would be stone cold until the ovens warmed the kitchen.

By the time she arrived at the shop, she'd warmed considerably.

"There are a couple of police cars sitting out front. The glass on the door is busted," James said as he pulled the vehicle to the curb.

Tension gripped her. They kept very little cash on the premises. The previous day's deposit had been delivered at the bank's overnight drop, so she wasn't concerned about that. But there were other things—heavy and expensive equipment, or any of the baked goods were just as valuable. What if any of the cakes or other candy creations had been damaged. Some of the more intricate pieces could not be duplicated in a matter of hours.

"Can you tell if someone has been in the shop, James?" She couldn't mask the anxiety from her voice.

"Not from here, Miss. Did you call Avery?" James turned off the car, exited and came around to her.

Penelope shivered from the sudden blast of air but was ready for it as James opened her door. "He'll probably be upset that I'm here and didn't wait."

"He takes his responsibility seriously. He knows how much this shop means to you." James gripped her elbow as she stepped from the vehicle. "Hold tight to my arm, Miss Penelope. Doesn't look like the city has shoveled or salted the walks yet."

She gripped his arm as they carefully moved forward. Snow crunched and skittered over her feet. A gust of arctic air cut through her thick layers, and she ducked her head.

"This is the worst part about being a baker—waking up in the middle of the night and getting bombarded by frigid air," she muttered.

James chuckled. "Yes, ma'am, much agreed." He paused. "There's a bit of glass here. Don't touch anything."

"Okay." She allowed herself to be maneuvered around the trouble area and into relative warmth. The hum of the refrigeration units were loud in the silent shop.

A hand gripped hers.

"Miss Bishop. Officer Rogers is here," a soft, almost feminine voice said.

"Oh. Hello."

"My partner is with your assistant. It appears most of the damage was to the door. Luckily, no one actually entered the shop, but they're checking to make sure."

"Okay. That doesn't sound too bad," Penelope said.

"Other businesses have been vandalized in the area over the last several weeks, and we're not quite sure as to why."

She could only nod at the information. Her shop wasn't in a bad part of town; on the contrary, it was in downtown Ann Arbor. The bakery drew patrons from the surrounding office buildings as well as the few hotels and local colleges nearby. Lots of people to keep the businesses thriving.

"I thought I heard you out here."

Penelope sucked in a gasp. Every time she heard her assistant's voice, she was reminded of aged whiskey, smooth and mellow. And a man with that type of dulcet tone must have a body to go with it. For a moment, she squashed the fantasy of running her hands over his sinewy flesh.

"Yes, I'm here."

"I was telling Officer Buck we're missing a few blocks of chocolate, and of course, the door."

She scratched her head. "Did you say chocolate?"

"Yeah. One dark, one milk, and two white."

"Give us a moment to assign you a claim number, then we'll get out of your way." That had to be the other officer. His voice was gravelly, like he was a heavy smoker.

Clothes rustled and static crackled as the officers scouted the shop's perimeter. Wind whipped against her ankles as they exited.

A throat cleared, and she turned to her left.

"If you don't mind, Miss Penelope, I'll help clean things a bit and make them safer for you to navigate," James said. "Everything else looks good around here."

A smile creased her lips. "Thank you, James."

"I've already filed a claim with our insurance company and hired someone to fix the front door." Avery grasped her hand and threaded it through the crook of his arm.

She hesitated, unused to the jolt of awareness sizzling up her arm.

"Something wrong?"

"I, uh... no." She allowed him to lead her forward. Their footsteps echoed, then were muffled on carpet. Only one place in the building contained carpet, and that was the corridor leading to the consultation rooms. "Any particular reason why you're dumping me in a consult room?"

"It's warmer up here, and you don't have to walk through a bunch of glass," Avery said. There was a catch in his voice.

She clutched his sleeve. "Is there something you're not telling me?"

"You're entirely too perceptive at times." He blew out a sigh. "I received a phone call the other day, asking if the shop was for sale."

"And you said?"

"The shop isn't for sale. What did you expect me to say? This is your family's business, and everyone knows it's not for sale."

She trailed her fingers along the smooth walls until they reached an opening. "But why would anyone think this business is for sale? We've been here for over a hundred years. We're not going anywhere."

"Right."

"So you're thinking the call and the break-in are related?"

"Maybe someone is trying to scare you into selling."

She snorted. "Like that would ever happen." She shrugged out of her coat. Before she could find the coat tree to hang it, Avery removed it from her fingers. Awareness zipped up her arm. Heat crept into her cheeks as once more desire sidled through her veins. "Thank you."

He halted before her. "You're not upset that I'm leaving you in here while we clean up the mess out there?"

She rested a hand on his chest. Warmth seeped through her palm. For a moment, she considered what it would be like to have it pressed to his skin. Would he have coarse or downy soft hair, or perhaps, none at all? Damn her dream. Swallowing hard, she dropped her hand. "I would be a higher liability out there. No sense in distracting you from what needs to be done."

"You keep things interesting." He tucked a curl behind her ear. "Your hair is wet."

"I know."

"You didn't have to come out. I could've handled this." Disapproval hung in his voice.

She lifted a defiant chin. "It's not your responsibility."

"But you are," he murmured. "I'll be back to get you when we're done."

Stunned, Penelope could only nod. When he said things like that, she got the impression she meant more to him than just a co-worker, but he couldn't be interested in her. At least, she didn't think he was. But then, why should he be?

The faint thud of his footfalls signaled his departure. Carefully, she made her way toward a chair and sat. On any other day, she'd be elbow deep in a bowl of cake batter or rolling out dough for pie crust. Everything in the shop was made from scratch. Everything from cookies to frosting to the limited selection of chocolate candies.

She dragged agitated fingers through her tangle of damp hair. If something more had been taken, then maybe she could see the rationale, but a few blocks of chocolate and a broken door were not enough to intimidate her.

And speaking of the door... She stood and made her way to the room entrance. With one hand on the door jamb, she stepped into the hall and listened to the sounds of the bakery.

The murmur of voices along with the tinkle of glass and the slight drag of straw strands against linoleum drifted to her ears. Beyond that, diesel engines grumbled while air brakes squealed. Soon, downtown would awaken, and though she wanted to open the shop for business, she had to be certain it was safe to do so.

As she stepped back into the room, her fingers fell on smooth cool paper. She peeled the page from its mooring on the wall, then slid her hand across the missive, surprised to find tiny raised dots—Braille. *This can't be right.*

She skimmed her fingers over the bumps again.

You are my everything.

Why would someone send her this? Could it be her mystery man? Hope surged anew. But how did he know where she worked?

She returned to the hall, this time walking until she stood at the edge where the carpet met the tile.

"Avery?" Cool air swirled around her ankles.

Footsteps shuffled, the squeak of hinges and his soft tread. "Yes?"

She held out the sheet of paper. "Have you seen this?"

"It's in Braille, honey," he said. "Where'd you find it?"

"Taped to the wall in the office."

"Maybe your parents had one of the employees put it up."

She shook her head. "This sounds like a love note or something."

"A love note?"

She could practically hear the smile vibrating in his voice. "Don't get any ideas. I have no one to send me love notes." The man she was dating had dumped her, or rather, she dumped him on New Year's Eve.

"What does it say?"

She huffed.

"C'mon, P. What's it say?"

"As much as you type up notes for me, you still haven't learned?"

He laughed, a warm throaty chuckle which reminded her of tempered chocolate. She wanted to hear that wonderful sound all day. He threaded her hand through the crook of his arm and led her back the way she came.

"What are you doing?"

"Checking to see if there are any more notes hanging on the walls. So spill. What does it say?"

"You are my everything."

"That's a lovely sentiment," he said.

"It is, but from whom?"

Avery paused. Paper rattled. "There's a rather crude drawing of a sandwich on the bottom." He grabbed her hand and placed it over the lines. "Looks like peanut butter and jelly."

She giggled.

"What's so funny?"

"That's a nickname my grandfather gave me as a kid and shortened it to P." She shook her head. A smile twisted her lips while her heart softened at the memory. She loved that gruff old man, now sitting on an island somewhere, ordering his nurse to bring him whatever the local flavor was. "He's way past retirement and urged my parents to turn the shop over to me. I know he didn't leave this note."

"Then you have a secret admirer."

"I doubt that."

"Why? It's the perfect time of year for it."

She shook her head, pursing her lips. There was no secret admirer for her. After the way things ended with Sam, she didn't want to think about anyone wooing her. Her ego hadn't quite recovered from the dent, even if her heart had.

"C'mon, P. You're the first one of us to celebrate the holiday. You love the idea of love."

"Didn't you get the memo? Valentine's is canceled this year due to a missing heart."

He chuckled. "That's funny. I'll have to use that sometime."

"I'm serious."

"I know." He pressed the paper into her hand. "Someone thinks you're everything to them. That's all that matters." A soft click filled the silence. "I don't see anything else. Maybe I should check the other rooms."

"I don't think that's necessary." She turned, reached out, but grasped only air.

"Nothing here, P." His voice was farther away, each of the other three doors opening and closing. A moment later, he returned to her side.

She shook her head. "After everything that's happened, it's just strange to find it in here."

"I'll keep an eye out for any other love notes and alert the staff."

She could just imagine what her employees would say about a secret admirer. At least, she wouldn't catch any speculative looks. Being blind did have its perks. "Maybe not the staff." She touched his sleeve. "They don't need to know."

"Whatever you say, P."

She went still as he leaned close. The subtle scent of his cologne enveloped her as easily as his heat.

"You're cute when you blush."

A faint breeze brushed her cheek, followed by fading footfalls. He was gone. Was he flirting with her? She had half a mind to call him back, but then, what? If she were wrong, she'd make a total fool of herself, and she'd had enough of that to last her the rest of the year.

Chapter Three

They didn't open for business, but Penelope had the bakers stay. They still had orders to fulfill even if they weren't waiting on new customers. The door was slowly being repaired, and the only heat in the building came from the bank of ovens. Every now and then cold air swirled through the room nipping at her ankles and toes.

She concentrated on the modeling chocolate she was manipulating into rose petals.

Well, at least *trying* to manipulate into rose petals. She rolled the mixture, then pinched off a pea-sized amount before flattening it between her thumb and forefinger. This bit was pliant like taffy. She then pinched off a larger piece, about the size of a quarter. But when she tried to shape it into a cone, the chocolate broke.

She tried again, retooling and reshaping, but with the same poor results.

With a huff, she tugged off one latex glove. *Let me try one more time.* She rolled the piece again and frowned.

"Dammit," she said, just as another crumbled in her hand. *The candy is too dry, making the flowers brittle.*

She slammed down the ruined chocolate and turned her attention toward the bowl. Then, she dumped out the container on her work surface. The whole batch felt crumbly, almost as if someone had left the top off or hadn't added enough liquid to the mixture. There must be a way to salvage this batch of candy.

The timer hummed, then buzzed.

Thankful for the distraction, she set her work aside and covered the chocolate with a damp cloth. She peeled off her other glove and grabbed a set of oven mitts. Shrill chiming split the air. The dang phone hadn't stopped ringing either.

"Hot swinging," she hollered to no one in particular. The last thing she wanted to do was burn one of her workers. The oven door slammed shut, and she carefully walked toward the cooling rack, then set down the tray of cakes.

"Penelope. Phone."

"I'll take it in my office." She tossed the mitts on the rack and headed for the swinging doors ten steps away. *I need a break from this task.*

It was much cooler back here, a welcome respite from the heat of the kitchen. Her footsteps echoed on the flat concrete. She fumbled with the doorknob on the left second door, then walked in and kicked it closed.

"Hello." The greeting came out slightly breathless.

"Hey… Am I catching you at a bad time?"

A smile curved her lips at the sound of her best friend's voice. "No, I was just pulling something out of the oven. What's up?"

"I just wanted to hear a friendly voice."

"Why? What happened? You did it, didn't you?"

"Did what?"

"The nasty with that detective."

"I did not!" Moira screeched.

Penelope chuckled. Her friend had been playing hard to get with a homicide detective but hadn't done more than kiss the man. "Maybe not, but you want to."

"This is not why I called you."

"Okay. So what else is happening?"

"Somebody took pot shots at me."

Penelope tensed. She knew her friend's work was sometimes dangerous, but to hear her casual statement of "pot shots," left her a little annoyed. "As in … shooting at you with a gun?"

"Yeah."

"You know, you and Violet will be the death of me one day as I sit here in my little bakery and succumb to a heart attack because my best friends are stupid!" Penelope yelled the last part. "I swear you do this for fun. You couldn't find a nice safe job somewhere. Not that that worked well for Violet. What do you two do, take out ads at Villains-R-Us with eight by ten glossies of yourselves? And asking, no—*begging* you to be careful is just… Are you even listening to me?" She huffed. "Do I need to come down there and—"

A knock interrupted her tirade.

"What?" she called, holding the phone away from her mouth.

"There's a delivery here, and Avery's dealing with the door guy," a feminine voice called.

"I'll be right there." Penelope returned to the phone. "Moira?" She listened to the background noises on the other end. Papers rustled and a muttered curse. "Moira!"

"Yeah. What."

Penelope rolled her eyes. "Will you stay out of trouble and try not to get shot at?"

"There's no fun in that. So tell me … how is Avery?"

That is a good question. She twirled the curly phone cord around her finger as she leaned back in her chair.

"Pens?" Moira said.

"He's fine."

More rattling and shuffling carried through the earpiece. *What is Moira doing?*

"Ya know, Pens, I've only talked to Avery on the phone when I'm looking for you, but I think I like your assistant more than I like the guy you were dating. But, hey, that's just my observation."

A loud snap startled her. "What was that?"

"What was what?" Moira asked.

"That sound."

Hesitation. "Oh, nothing. I have to go, but I'll call you later."

"You better." Penelope dropped the phone into its cradle, then rubbed her temples. She knew her BFF was up to something, but she'd have to wait for a phone call.

She almost went to call Violet, to see what she had going on, when she grasped the watch on her wrist. *Darn, this thing isn't working again. It is probably too early to call her anyway.* That was another thing. Why did Moira ask about Avery? Ever since she told Moira and her other best friend, Violet, about that New Year's Eve kiss, they had both insisted the mystery man was Avery.

Penelope doubted that. Avery always maintained his professionalism. Though, it did seem like he was flirting with her earlier. Then again, she was still coasting from her vivid sex dream.

She stood, walked to the door, twisted it open, then stepped into the hall.

No additional cold air. No rumble of a diesel engine idling, nor the squeak of a pallet jack. Had she missed the delivery? She listened to the sounds of the bakery for a little longer. A short bark of laughter drifted above the whine of a power drill. The clang of metal against metal told her everything was normal. Even the ol' school playing on the radio was normal.

"In other news," the DJ began. "The body of small business owner, Dicky Williams was found mutilated inside his business. Williams, the owner of Dicky's A/V Showroom was forty-six years old. The police are asking anyone with information to please contact them."

Penelope sighed. *What a loss.* Not that she was a huge fan of Williams, but he had helped install some of the smart features in the bakery. *He will be missed.*

She moved forward and slowly entered the bakery kitchen. Heat enveloped her in its warm embrace. "Shay, I thought you said there was a delivery?"

"Front counter," the young woman said. "I'd grab it, but I'm elbow deep in cheesecake."

"I can get it." Penelope zigged and zagged her way through the maze of tables and pushed through the low swinging doors. The drone of the power drill ceased. After all the noise, the silence was unsettling.

A faint mint smell wafted in the air. She sniffed and stepped forward.

"Penelope, stop," Avery ordered.

She stood still. Footsteps scratched across the floor, followed by the scrape of something metallic. Something brushed her face, and she held her breath.

A warm chuckle slid down her spine, tightening her nipples.

She gasped. She knew that sound. In her excitement, she forgot Avery's order to not move and stepped forward. Something rounded but sharp grazed her temple, leaving a burning sensation in its wake.

"Penelope." Equal measures of exasperation and concern clung to his smooth baritone.

Metal clattered to her right. She pressed her fingertips to her head, and they came away damp. "Great. Just great," she muttered.

"Is she okay?" This came from across the room.

"Yeah." Avery stepped close, his hands on her shoulders.

When he leaned closer, she held her breath. Awareness crackled through her veins. She clutched her hands at her side. What was wrong with her? Being this close to Avery had never produced this type of reaction before. Why now?

She slowly exhaled. *It is probably all that pent-up sexual energy and nightly erotic dreams messing with her senses.*

"Why did you move?"

"I thought someone else was here," she said, just as his fingers brushed her hair from her face.

"You should put antiseptic on that and keep it covered." He tucked a curl behind her ear. "Who did you think was here?"

She opened her mouth but quickly closed it. Heat cruised her cheeks. It was bad enough she smacked her head, but if her mystery man was here and witnessed the whole thing, she'd die of embarrassment. "Shay said I had a delivery."

"Avoidance?"

"You should try it sometime."

"Uh-huh. Stay put."

She touched her head again.

"And leave that alone. You're worse than a two-year-old sometimes," Avery admonished. Plastic rattled, and the sound grew closer. "Hold this."

She held out her hands and was mildly surprised when something heavy rested on her palms. She tightened her grip, plastic rustling. Balancing the gift with one hand, she explored with the other. The container wasn't that big. No longer than a loaf of bread but twice as wide. Maybe a basket of some sort. Through the thin plastic, her fingers discerned the shape of cylindrical bottles and something scrunchy.

Gentle pressure built where she'd scratched her head. Something cool briefly dabbed at the cut before it erupted into fiery pain. She sucked a breath through clenched teeth and jerked away. Avery held her fast.

"What the heck was that?" she demanded when he finally released her.

"That was antiseptic," he replied, a hint of amusement in his voice. "Did that hurt?"

She frowned. "Worse than hitting my head. Don't ever do that again," she said as she tried to swipe at her head, but he grabbed her wrist, stopping her.

"Then next time, if I say be still, do it."

A shiver of desire tiptoed down her spine at the quiet command. How often had she heard those words uttered in her dreams? She swallowed several times, hoping to regain what little control she had over her errant thoughts.

"What's that look?" Avery asked

"What look?"

"The one on your face."

"Why don't you tell me? It's not like I can see my own expression," she quipped.

Avery laughed. "Right. Right."

She tilted her head. "So what's in the basket?" She brought it closer to her nose and sniffed. Faint scents of lavender and mint wafted into her nostrils. "It smells divine, but I doubt it's edible."

"No, it isn't edible. Seems you've got everything you need for a luxurious bath."

Pleasure stole through her. "How nice." A long soak in the tub after getting home would be the perfect way to end her day. "Is there a card?"

An envelope was then pressed into her hand after the basket was removed.

Curious, she slipped the small stiff paper from the envelope and drifted her fingers over the front. Again, tiny raised dots met her sensitive fingertips.

Enjoy something steamy.

Heat flushed her cheeks. There wasn't a name at the bottom. She extended the card toward Avery. "Is it signed?"

"Sorry, P. Just another sandwich drawing."

She nodded. "Okay. I'm guessing all of this is leading to some sort of big reveal with Valentine's Day being what… three days away?"

"Yes, three days."

"All right." She tucked the gift under her arm and carefully made her way toward the swinging double doors. "Tell James I'll meet him in the back."

"Will do."

"Yoo-hoo," a masculine voice called. "Penelope? Are you in here?"

Penelope smiled. "Swift. How lovely to *see* you."

"Hello, my dear," Swift greeted. "I stopped by to see how you were doing and to possibly grab a cookie."

"Hey, Swift." Avery removed the basket from Penelope's hands and set it on the back counter.

"We're not open at the moment, but Avery will bring a few treats so we can catch up."

"Sure thing, P," Avery said.

The swinging doors announced his departure. Penelope threaded her arm through Swift's and led him to one of the consult rooms.

She liked the older gentleman whose daytime profession was a private investigator, while at night he worked as a semi-pro wrestler.

She squeezed his rock-hard biceps. "You're working out again."

"Yeah. I'm gearing up for the upcoming Iron Man contest. I gotta show these younger guys how it's done."

"Any juicy cases you can dish? My friend, Moira, is a private detective in Florida, and she's always busy or in trouble."

Swift laughed. "I don't know how juicy, but I did want to make certain you were being careful."

"About what?" When they'd reached the room, they parted ways for side-by-side chairs.

"Did you hear about the A/V company murder?"

"Yes. It's simply horrible."

"The family asked me to look into it."

"We have peanut butter, and oatmeal raisin," Avery announced as he entered. "There's also coffee and tea."

"Avery!" Swift said suddenly.

"Yes, sir?"

"Don't *sir* me," Swift admonished. Fabric rustled as he shifted forward. Paper crinkled, and the plate scratched, indicating he had grabbed a cookie from the plate. "You keep an extra careful eye on our Penelope."

"I always do, Swift."

"Don't patronize an old man. I'm very serious."

Penelope frowned. "Perhaps you should explain."

Swift sighed. "It's just a feeling I have. When I walked by the crime scene, the police wouldn't allow me in just yet. Then, I got a flash that this killer is on a mission, and he doesn't plan to stop at one."

"Swift has a touch of ESP or clairvoyance," Penelope explained. "He's a pretty good psychic detective."

"It comes in handy now and then," Swift agreed. "Father Time Detective Agency at your service. We don't stand around and make faces."

They groaned at the pun.

"With that, I will go check on the work and make sure we've completed all of today's orders."

"Oh, Avery?" Penelope called. "Did we get an order from Vector Integrated Practices? They usually order tarts and candies for the office and clients, but I haven't seen anything come across my desk?"

"I'll double check." With that, the door closed.

"Stick close to that young man, Penelope."

She smiled. "He's definitely a keeper."

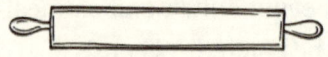

Sam Davis hurried up the rock salt strewn walk and pounded on the front door. He glanced around the snow-covered yard with some envy. The large two-story home lounged far enough from the road to give it privacy and plenty of lawn to enjoy in the summer. Now there were mounds and mounds of undisturbed white. He stepped back, craning his neck for a glimpse of any light behind the curtained windows. Not a single stingy sliver of light could be seen.

White smoke puffed and billowed above a chimney, the only indication someone could be inside. He lifted his hand and banged the door again.

Locks snapped and the door opened to a young, pretty, but flustered woman.

"May I-?"

Sam pushed past her into the warm foyer. "I'm here for Penny," he announced loosening his scarf.

Annoyance flickered in her brown eyes. "Miss Penelope isn't home yet." She glanced at the hall clock. "She should be here soon. I'm afraid I can't invite you in further," she said in a tone that didn't indicate remorse at all.

Sam sniffed. "Whatever. I'll be right here when she arrives," he said dismissively.

With a shrug, the young woman turned and walked into another room off the hall.

Sam gazed around the hall, or was it a foyer? Whatever it was soared the height of the house. A wide sweeping staircase rose to the second floor. He could just make out the landing and the hall beyond.

He focused his attention on the downstairs. The white marble flooring with its veins of blues and pinks was covered in a flowered beige nonskid runner. The accent table with its spill of mums and carnations added a pleasant and fragrant touch to the entry way.

And all of this could've been his.

He pulled off his gloves and stuffed them in his pockets. Had he been a little more patient or used a bit more finesse, he could've been spending his nights here. He could've possibly moved in, and this beautiful old home could've been his. The intricate crown molding, crystal chandelier, spacious rooms. He walked to the edge of the runner. The marble carried down the long hall to end in closed doors. The only opening was the dining room to his right. From previous visits he knew the pocket doors could be closed leaving the occupants to a quiet dinner. Just the right touch for a man such as himself to impress colleagues and clients.

A home like this was wasted on a woman who couldn't see its magnificence or truly appreciate the architectural majesty.

Had he been a little more discreet and not flaunted Shelia on New Year's Eve he would be in this beautiful home with its servants.

Penelope would never think of that young woman and the old people as servants. They were her friends and family. He sneered at the idea. Those people were paid to take care of Penelope, and that made them servants.

He stalked to an oil painting hanging opposite the stairs. He studied it a moment, trying to decipher the meaning of the frothy white capped waves and a jaunty little sailboat barely managing to stay out of reach of a black, towering wave.

A faint whir caught his attention and he looked up and around for the source of the sound. A camera mounted high on the ceiling tracked his movements. He was certain if he strayed too far from the entryway some other servant would have him thrown out.

He continued studying the flowers and the ornate mirror near the front door. The walls had been painted a soft shade of peach, which was carried into the pattern of the skid-proof runner. He did another slow circle and realized what was missing. The little oversized bench. It had been replaced with the accent table.

His gaze wandered to the gleaming wood steps with some disdain. He looked at his wool slacks and the sharp crease. There was no way he was going to sit on a riser like an ordinary person. He would just have to wait standing up. He glanced at the hall clock. A smirk curved his lips. She should be home any minute. It wasn't like she opened for business today. He'd seen to that. But was it enough to force her back into his arms?

Keys jangled, and the knob wiggled. Well there was only one way to find out.

Sam was waiting for her when she arrived home nearly an hour later. Quick falling snow left the roads hazardous, and the driving was slow. By the time James escorted her into the welcome warmth of the foyer, she was more than ready to try out her new bath products.

The faint scent of jasmine and spicy musk alerted her she wasn't alone in the hall. Fabric swishing and the squeak of shoes confirmed it.

"Penny," Sam said.

She stifled a groan. "Who let you in here?"

"Um… some young lady. I threw myself on her good graces." He cupped her shoulders and leaned down.

Penelope shifted, raised her hands, and shoved him away. "I want you out of here." She reached a hand out before her. "Mrs. Tilman," she called. "Mrs. Tilman!" The woman was always around, and if she let him in the house, they were going to have words. *Wait.* Did he just say, *young lady?*

"Honestly, Penny. Can't we just let bygones be bygones?"

Footsteps beat a hasty staccato on the wood. A waft of vanilla teased her nostrils. Let bygones be bygones indeed.

"I'm more than willing to let that happen, but you keep turning up."

"Miss Penelope." The voice was young and a bit breathless. "My mother got called away and told me to stay until she returned."

"Kassie." Kassie was Mrs. Tilman's youngest daughter, and she often helped when she was home from school. "Oh, no. Is everything all right?" Penelope allowed the young woman to help her from her coat.

"Oh, yes. My brother locked his keys in the car, and the company won't release the vehicle without her signature."

"And what's the story with … my guest?"

"I—he arrived shortly after mom left," Kassie said, her tone a bit strained.

Sam huffed. "I'm standing right here."

"I'm aware of where you're standing. You're wearing that hideous leather jacket, and Sheila's perfume. Did you want something in particular, or were you just in the neighborhood?"

"I heard about the break-in at the bakery and wanted to make sure you were okay."

The lack of concern in his voice was underwhelming and did little to convince her that he was there for her well-being. No, something else was on his agenda. "I'm just fine. You may leave."

Shuffling feet reached her ears. "Kassie, please show Sam the door. He has more than overstayed his welcome."

"I came here out of the goodness of my heart, and you are treating me like trash."

"I seriously doubt you have a heart. Why are you really here, Sam? We both know I'm not your ideal woman, let alone in a professional setting, for a man of your intellect."

Kassie's muffled cough almost covered her blurted giggle.

"You are just ungrateful."

"I've been called worse. Leave my home and never return."

"You'll regret throwing me out."

"Actually, Sam, I feel pretty damn good about it."

Cold blasted the entryway, and she shivered. Grumbling drifted to her ears, then Kassie's light tread and Sam's heavier one. The door slammed shut, and warmth returned to the foyer.

"I'm sorry, Miss Penelope. I had no idea—"

She held up a hand, cutting off the apology. "It's okay." She allowed Kassie to lead her into the dining room. "How's school?"

"I got the surgical residency at the hospital."

"Fantastic news. We should celebrate."

"Sleep is celebration for me." They paused, and Kassie placed Penelope's hand on the back of a rounded wood chair. "That's a beautiful basket, and it smells heavenly."

Penelope felt for the table, and placed her gift on the surface before sitting down. "A gift. I have a secret admirer."

"Oh, how romantic." Awe filled Kassie's voice. "Mom told me about your mystery man from New Year's Eve. Do you think he sent this to you?"

"I'm not sure. For a second, I thought he was in the shop today before I smacked my head into something."

"Oh, dear."

She chuckled. "I'm fine."

"How does Avery feel about the gifts?" A drawer opened and closed; silverware rattled. A moment later, a woven placemat and cutlery was placed before her.

"Avery?" Penelope smoothed out the cloth before arranging the knife, fork, and spoon in alinement with the bottom edge of the placemat.

Kassie tapped her hand with a linen napkin. Penelope folded this in half, then thirds, before setting it to the right of her fork.

"He goes all soft when you're in the room," Kassie admitted.

"He seemed happy about it."

"Uh-huh." A glass thunked down near Penelope's left hand as Kassie said, "And how do you feel about Avery?"

The question caught her off guard, but the answer must have shown on her face.

"Interesting. I'll bring your dinner. Mom made meatloaf. Said you might need some comfort food this evening."

Penelope's lips curved upward. "She's right."

"I'll go check on dinner."

"I'll be in my office. I need to check on something Avery mentioned earlier."

The familiar scent of orange, lemon, and various wood undertones helped ease the tension from her body. She didn't need her cane here. Each room held a different scent and texture. The furniture seldom moved, and she had a housekeeper/live-in assistant who helped with the day-to-day running of her home—thanks to her parents.

That was the only way they would allow her to live on her own. She was grateful for her parents, but sometimes they worried too much, just like her best friends. The only way she could prove to any of them that she was capable of living a full and productive life was to work in the family business, PB & J Bakery.

Dinner could wait a moment. *I need to check a few things on my computer.* With ease, she moved down a hallway, then twisted the knob on the third door to her right. As a house rule, doors were left closed, making it less likely for her to run into one.

She crossed the threshold. The scent of aged leather and fruitwood greeted her. Six paces to the high back executive chair, she eased into the seat and swung it around until her legs were beneath the desk. Carefully, she skimmed her hands over the surface. Sometimes, Mrs. Tilman liked to leave mail scattered on the desk, her way of keeping Penelope on her toes. Finding none, she grabbed the small headset beside the keyboard and slipped it over her head.

Using voice commands, she opened her web browser and listened as each email recipient was read to her. She rolled her eyes at the numerous messages from dating sites. How did those keep slipping into her inbox when she seldom surfed the Internet?

"Delete last five messages," she commanded. "Continue." She blinked. "Rewind and replay." *That can't be right.*

She listened again, turning the volume up.

"To proceed with this transfer, please re-type your security code. If you've received this message in error, please—"

Penelope snatched off the headset and scrambled for the phone. If there was anyone who could help fix this mess, it would be Violet. She hastily punched in the numbers and listened to the ringing on the other end. "C'mon. C'mon. Pick up." The phone then answered on the fourth ring. "Violet? Are you busy?"

"What's up, P? You sound upset."

"Uh, just walked in the door and then had to have Sam thrown out. Then, I get an email from the bank about a transfer. I don't know what's going on. You know my bank isn't user friendly."

Violet chuckled.

Penelope listened. Clicking. She frowned, trying to decipher the sound. *Ahh.* Fingers hitting a keyboard came through loud and clear.

"I think I got it. Someone has been trying to access your account. Almost transferred all the bakery's capital into another account."

"Oh, my God."

"Don't get your thong in a twist. I canceled it and changed your password. It's a good thing you called me."

Relief sagged her shoulders, and she exhaled. "Thanks, Vee. You're a lifesaver."

"Anytime, P. Happy to help." Now that the disaster had been averted, her friend didn't sound so cheery.

"What's the matter with you? Lemme guess. You and Francis aren't bumping pelvises anymore?"

"Is 'bumping pelvises' a technical term? Or something they teach you in the baking business?" She sighed. "Why is there this sudden interest in my love life? And when did it became a federal offense to accept a damn cup of coffee? It wasn't even a large."

Penelope swallowed a giggle. "You're upset over coffee?"

"A girl needs her caffeine; the earlier, the better."

"I'm in total agreement with that, but it sounds like you need more than just java. You need a double shot."

"More like a double-barreled shotgun. Don't start with me, Penelope. It's bad enough Moira left a message about washing machine sex."

Now, she burst out laughing. "I knew it!"

A chuckle drifted through the line. "I know, I know. Wonder if it was during the spin cycle."

A slow hiss, like steam being released, filled the remaining silence.

"You're at the coffee shop?"

"Jeez, P. You don't miss a trick. Now this bank thing… focus on what's important."

"You already took care of that. Now my focus is on coffee. You. Upset. Coffee guy must be flirting with you again." Rustling clothes and the quiet squeak of a chair filled the momentary silence.

"Penelope, I promise… if you mention my love life one more time, I'll send your parents pictures from our trip to Mardi Gras. I'm sure they'd love to see those."

She sucked in a breath, her cheeks aflame from the very fuzzy memories of beads and sexy men from freshman year. "So what's the problem?"

Violet chuckled. "Much better."

Penelope rubbed her temple. *First Sam. Now this?* "Thanks, Violet."

"It was a pretty juvenile attempt. Woulda worked too if they weren't forced to put in a second password." Metallic scraping screeched through the line. "For God's sake, what is he doing here?"

"Who?"

More scraping, then rustling. Raised voices echoed through earpiece. "Oh, this is going to get ugly and fast. I'll call you later. Oh. Wait. You find your mystery man yet?"

"No, but he's still leaving me gifts."

"Sweet." A loud crash echoed through the line. "Later."

Penelope lowered the handset. Why did she have the sneaking suspicion that Sam was behind the attempted theft?

Forty-five minutes later, Penelope eased into fragrant, swirling water. She sank into her bath until the water reached her chin, and her head leaned against the bath pillow. A long sigh escaped her lips as the tension drained from her limbs. The jets buffeted her body, and she inhaled the sweet scent of lavender and mint.

She lifted one hand from the water and carefully slid her fingers along the lip of the tub until she found her glass of wine. She raised the flute to her lips. The cool fruity liquid splashed over her tongue and trickled down her throat.

With each swallow, she released the stresses of her day. The door was repaired. Business would resume as usual. Sam was his usual asinine self. How dare he show up at her house. She took another sip of wine, savoring the slightly mellow flavor. Other than the gifts, one of which she was enjoying at the moment, her mind fluttered to Avery.

Oh, she still thought about her mystery man, but Avery was always there for her, looking out for her well-being. Even when she scratched her head. He didn't have to treat the wound with careful attention, but he did. And it reminded her so much of her New Year's Eve dance partner.

And then, he had said two magic words: Be still. Just replaying that moment made her nipples stiff and desire pulse between her legs. Once the thought took hold, it was hard to dislodge as she set her now empty glass down with a clink.

She so wanted to ask him if he'd punish her if she moved again, but it didn't quite seem appropriate. Still, his melodious voice echoed in her head, replacing her mystery man's hoarse whisper.

She drifted her hands down her body, pretending they were Avery's.

Her nipples stood erect, just above the swirling water. Cool air racing over the taut peaks provided a sensual contrast of eroticism. She grazed her palm over the tip, savoring the spark zinging from tit to clit. There, she lingered, building her desire until a sigh parted her lips. One hand dipped below the surface and delved into her folds. She allowed her legs to fall open, her knees resting against the tub walls as she traced her swollen nether lips.

She circled her clit before plunging a finger into her tight channel. It had been way too long since she had sex or even given herself special attention. Between the relaxing scent of lavender, the heated embrace of the water, and the glass of wine, she welcomed this bit of self-love.

She alternated between the taut peaks of her breasts, tugging and twisting the sensitive nips while stroking and pushing at her clit. She added another finger for good measure, her hips moving with each thrust of her hand.

Her soft moans echoed off the tiles, getting lost in the hum of the jets. Tension coiled in her stomach, waiting for release. She shifted in the tub, and pressurized water drifted over her mound. She left her breasts long enough to reposition the spray to hit her sensitized bud with each roll of her hips.

Sweat beaded on her forehead and rolled down her face. She used both hands now, three fingers pumped inside her pussy while she rolled that hardened bundle of nerves with the other. Water sloshed over the side of the tub as she moved faster. Her world narrowed to the silvery sensations rippling through her body, then she was sliding. She cried out as her orgasm crashed over her, starlight bursting behind her lids. Her pussy clenched and pulsed around her fingers. She slowed each stroke, riding the climax as long as she could, until drifting on a wave of complete bliss.

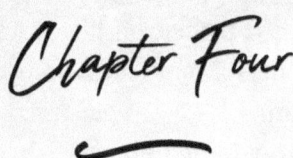

Chapter Four

Two days until Valentine's Day, and Penelope wasn't sure if she was excited or dreading the holiday. Maybe dreading it a little. The holiday was for lovers and sweethearts, and she had neither this year. Well, not entirely true. Someone was sending her gifts and love notes.

Her hand clutched the smooth handle of her spatula as she gritted her teeth. On the ride in, her driver, James, gabbed incessantly about his plans with his wife. She was happy for him—them—but she didn't want to hear anything more about Valentine's Day. It only increased her anxiety about who was sending her those anonymous gifts.

And someone who knew her was sending them. How else would they know to put the cards in Braille? Gifts aside, she still had a business to run. And after yesterday's confusion, she'd forgotten one of today's orders.

Cold air swirled around her ankles as a door scraped closed.

Penelope lifted her head, listening. Soft shoes slapped against the hard cement floor. Hinges squeaked, and she caught the whiff of a woodsy cologne.

A smile teased her lips, and she fumbled for the damp towel she'd placed on her workstation. Gentle hands covered hers a moment before the towel settled in her right palm.

"What are you doing here so early?"

Penelope wiped her hands, using the time to savor the low timbre of Avery's voice. Lately, listening to his dulcet tones conjured satin sheets and steamy bubble baths. Heat crept into her cheeks. *Definitely baths.*

"I came in to work on paperwork, then realized we'd forgotten an order for ten dozen chocolate-covered cherries."

"So you thought you'd start without me?" A teasing note clung to his question.

"Then you should get in a little earlier." The towel was removed from her hand and something small and rectangular landed in its place.

"Right. I found this sticking out of the mailbox this morning."

She turned the object over in her hand, running her fingertips over the smooth wrapping before she encountered a narrow strip of cloth. Not cloth, ribbon. It felt like a jewelry box, but who would send her that kind of gift? Her birthday was still several months away.

"Are you sure this is for me? It feels like a present, and well…"

"Give me your finger."

Without hesitation, she complied.

Avery guided her digit to a stiff tag and raised dots. "What does it say?" he asked as he pressed closer. The heat of his body and the spicy scent of his cologne enveloped her, momentarily distracting her from the box in her hand.

She bit her lip as pleasure stole through her. "It has my name on it, but not who it's from."

"Well, open it."

Curiosity piqued, Penelope carefully peeled away the ribbon and paper until the slightly ridged box beneath surfaced. She still found it a little disconcerting that someone thought enough about her to send anonymous gifts.

Delight stole through her. *It is probably one of my regular customers.*

The wrapping was plucked from her fingers so she could concentrate on prying open the lid. Once removed, she encountered a small metal square with a tiny, blunted spike. She followed it over the textured leather to an oblong face. Raised numbers greeted her fingertips while a slight ticking sound reached her ears.

"A watch?" She couldn't keep the awe from her voice. "Someone sent me a watch?"

"Looks like it. Oh, check this out." He grabbed her finger and placed it over a tiny button.

A mechanical voice announced the time. "A talking watch!" She giggled. This was the best thing ever, especially since her other one broke. "This is so great. Is there a card inside?" She proffered the box.

Scratching, then silence. "Nothing, P. Your secret admirer really likes you."

She snorted. "I highly doubt that, but it would be nice to know who sent me the watch, just so I can thank them."

"Oh wait. Here's something." Avery pushed stiff paper in her hand. "It's in Braille."

Penelope skimmed her fingers over the card. Her brow knitted. "This can't be right."

"Why? What does it say?"

"Someone went through a lot of trouble to do this." She shook her head. "You don't just switch the keyboard to type little dots. It's a special machine or at least a tool. And this watch? It's not something you pick up from the local Fossil store. It has to be ordered."

He chuckled.

"What's so funny?"

"You, Penelope. Can't you just enjoy a random anonymous gift?" He grabbed her wrist and settled the watch on her arm. The metal was cold as it touched her skin. The slide of his fingers on her flesh sent shivers of awareness down her spine.

"This isn't random. First the note, then the bath stuff. Now this? I just want to know who sent it."

"Does the card say anything?"

"All will be revealed on Valentine's Day."

Avery chuckled. "Well, then there's your answer."

She shook her head as he lowered her arm. Now she felt a bit bereft without his touch. "I just…" She sighed. "Want to know. What if it's from Sam?"

Avery coughed. "I doubt he'd ever put that much thought into anyone or anything but himself."

A frown tugged at the corners of her mouth, hearing the edge in Avery's voice. "You never said you didn't like him."

"Maybe if I'd met Sam in a different place, we'd hang out, but I didn't like the way he treated you. Especially after…" He coughed. "Well, after what you told me."

Penelope nodded. "Yeah. You're right."

Avery touched her hand. "You're better off without him." He threaded her arm through his and led her through the double doors back to her office. "I believe you have some invoices requiring your attention."

She paused on the threshold, sniffing. The scent of something sweet and exotic reached her nostrils. She inhaled appreciatively. "Is there someone else here?"

"No. Why?"

"I smell perfume."

He led her to the desk and placed her hand on the edge. She ran her fingers over the surface until she reached something cold and bubbled. Not bubbled, beveled, like glass. She followed the cool exterior to the wide rim. Something tickled her wrist, and she flinched.

God, I hope it isn't a bug. But she wasn't going to lose it, not with Avery standing a few feet behind her.

A heavy sigh eased from her lips. *Not a bug, thank goodness, but fronds and leaves.* Farther upward, she touched petals, circling her finger around the tight bloom, then bringing one to her nose. Yes, this was the source of the perfume. So beautiful.

She glanced over her shoulder. "What color are they?"

"Some are pink while others are a peachy-red. The one in your hand is pink, though."

His voice sounded a bit gruff to her ears, but she dismissed it as she felt for the plastic spindle normally associated with flowers. Finding none, she gave up.

"Is there a card?" she asked.

"On the vase."

She found the card. This one was also in Braille.

Until tonight, Your Secret Admirer.

"You're closing with me tonight, right?" She couldn't mask the nervous quiver of her voice.

"Yeah. Why?"

"This card says my secret admirer will be here tonight."

"Friend or foe, I'll protect you."

She nodded. "Hey, Avery."

"Yeah?"

"Thanks for everything. I know it can't be easy working with me all the time."

"No, but you do keep things interesting. I'm leaving now."

She listened to the soft slap of his shoes as he walked away. For the first time since she lost her vision, she wished she could see his butt. Because she knew he had to have a great butt to compliment his biceps.

She shook herself. She had no business thinking about her assistant in such a way. Yet, it would be interesting to see what he looked like, even if only with her fingertips.

That brought another matter. Who was sending her these gifts?

The hum of voices filled the air, blending with the whirl of the commercial mixer, punctuated by the intermittent shrill of oven timers.

"I just took out the last batch of cupcakes for that order. We've still got six more trays of cookies working," Shay said as she breezed by. "Stay still, P. Putting a hot tray on the cooling rack."

Penelope nodded and stepped forward. Heat flared at her back, then on her right side near her cheek. A squeak of wheels signaled as the long cooling rack was pushed away from her workstation.

"You know, it's been a year since I walked into that rack," she pointed out.

"You walked into a ladder yesterday. So I'm not taking any chances," Shay said, briefly standing beside Penelope. "I swear you can see something. There are award-winning pastry chefs who can't do what you do with two eyes and glasses."

She laughed and continued to scoop chocolate into waiting forms. These little truffle delights were going atop the cupcakes that had just been pulled from the oven. Along with a decadent icing and chocolate ganache. A true indulgent treat on Valentine's Day.

"Will these get tiny chocolate curls?"

"Nope, just truffles and icing. Avery will handle the detail work."

"Do you miss it?"

"Hmm?"

"Your vision."

Penelope set down her scoop. "Only when I'm feeling sorry for myself. Other than that, no."

"What about your reflection or a sunset or some hottie's delicious abs?"

She faced her co-worker. "What's up? What's with all the questions about my vision?"

"I..." She heard the hesitation in her voice. "Well..."

"Are you having problems?"

"Not at the moment, but eyes are a funny thing. One minute they're fine and the next ... they glaze over. Someone else has to drive me around. The last time I drove, my vision totally gave out."

"I'm so sorry to hear that, Shay. It's been so long since I lost my sight I don't even think about it anymore. It's become a part of who I am. And my life is quite full." She grinned. "I own this bakery, have friends, go out, even on dates and such."

"And you're not angry?"

"No, only when something stupid happens like ... walking into a door or when someone tries to take advantage of me." Penelope rested a hand on the table.

"I can give you the name of my counselor. She was very helpful with everything I needed."

"This might sound stupid, but … you're not going to fire me, are you?"

"Wow. Then those rumors of me being heartless would be true."

Shay laughed. "I told you it was stupid."

"Not stupid. It's a valid question, and one you never have to worry about here. Well, unless you start smuggling products out the back door or stealing cash from the register."

"Penelope, there's someone here to see you," a voice called from the front.

"Keep me posted, and let the rest of the staff know. We're real supportive around here." She peeled off her gloves, walked to the sink and washed her hands. "I'm wanted now." She pulled her cane from her pocket. With a flick of her wrist, it extended.

She continued through the maze of tables and through the half double doors that led to the front.

The tip of her cane met an obstruction. She paused, the doors smacking her butt on their outward swing. She moved upward until her hand touched the display case.

A hand covered hers, and she went still. "Hi," she greeted. Not sure who touched her, but it was definitely a large hand, a man's hand if she was right.

"You're looking radiant, as always, Penelope."

A tremor stole through her, and she snatched her hand away. She firmed her lips at the deep voice. *Again?* "Sam, what are you doing here?"

"You sound like you're still a little peeved. Is there somewhere we can talk? In private?"

Warm musk enveloped her before a hand slid down the curve of her spine, settling at the small of her back. "Everything okay?"

Penelope half turned. "Avery? You remember Sam?"

"I do."

The chill in her assistant's voice was unmistakable. "The assistant, right?"

"Right," Avery said. "Is there something I can help you with?"

"Just a private place to chat with Penny here."

Penelope shuddered at the hated nickname. She had never understood why he insisted on calling her that. With one hand on the display case and her cane in the other, she followed around the furniture to the end, then pushed open the waist-high half door.

"Let's talk in one of the consult rooms, Sam." Even as she crossed the showroom floor, she could feel the weight of Avery's stare. *What is with him?* The tap-tap-tap of the cane echoed off the linoleum, then hollowed as she neared the hallway that led to the consult rooms.

"Do you have to use that thing?" The quiet disapproval in his voice rang loud and clear.

She frowned. "Really? Would you prefer I run into something or someone?" She kept her tone light but infused enough annoyance to let him know she didn't like his question.

"I've never seen you use that in the shop."

"That's because the shop is open, and there are people walking around. It makes it easier for all parties involved." She paused at an open door, felt the wall inside and flicked on a light. For a moment, she blinked at the sudden change, but her world returned to darkness. "C'mon in and have a seat." She folded the cane, dropped it in her pocket and made her way around the desk.

"You have really done well for yourself."

"You sound like you expected me to fail, Sam." The chair springs squeaked as it accommodated her weight. "Why are you here? After last night, I thought I made it very clear ... I no longer wanted anything to do with you."

"I was wrong."

She settled on the edge of the chair, her palms flat against the smooth surface of the desk as she turned her head in his general direction. "Were you?" *I don't believe that for a moment.* He wasn't even looking at her but speaking down to the desk. "You can't even look at me when you talk to me."

"What? How do you know that? You can't even see." Surprise made his voice an octave higher.

"The direction of your voice. I'm blind, not stupid." She inhaled, using the time to settle her nerves. "Why are you here?"

The chair creaked beneath his weight, a whisper of clothing, then his hand covered hers. "I miss you."

Her laugh was brittle as she pulled her hand away, but he continued to hold on. "I sincerely doubt that.

What's the matter? Sheila doesn't like moving to first chair?"

"You were good to me."

"I was, and you disrespected me at every turn." She succeeded in jerking her hand from his. "Spare me. You said, and I quote, 'I don't have the patience to care for someone of such high maintenance.'" She stood. "My sight is not coming back, Sam. This isn't something that can be fixed, or a specialist can cure. I will be blind for the rest of my life."

"Penelope, I didn't mean it like that."

"Then how did you mean it? Because, to me, it sounds and feels like you want a perfect woman, one who doesn't have any physical defects. And you introduced her to me on New Year's, thinking I wouldn't notice her perfume all over your clothes." She shook her head. Anger replaced whatever hurt she'd harbored. "I need to return to work." She stood and maneuvered around the desk.

He caught her hand as she passed. "C'mon, Penny."

"I hate that name. Why do you insist on calling me that?" She snatched her hand away.

He cupped her cheek. "Because I like it, and your hair reminds me of a copper penny."

She huffed. "Don't call me that again. I hate that name. As a matter of fact, don't come to my shop again."

"Then sell me the shop."

"What?" There was no way she had heard him correctly. She could've sworn he just asked her to sell him the shop.

"Sell me this run-down bakery."

"It isn't for sale."

"You're making things very difficult. Downtown is a very lucrative area and a prime location for my investors. Name your price, Penny. I can make you a very rich woman."

She paused. Realization dawned, and it fueled her temper. "You only dated me to get my shop. What a prick. I bet you're behind that wannabe break-in yesterday, too." She planted her fists on her hips, if only to keep from hitting him. "This place will never be for sale, so take your offer and your investors and shove it."

A knock on the door drew her attention. "P? You all right?" The scent of Avery's cologne drifted to her.

"Would you show Sam out, please? He's not to return."

"Penny."

"She really detests that name," Avery said. "This way."

"But I'm trying to help you out."

Penelope firmed her lips. "I don't need or want your help."

"You remember that when someone comes to tear this place down. You'll regret you didn't stay with me."

"I regret having *met* you, Sam. Don't ever come back here and threaten me again."

"It's not a threat, Penny. I will watch your precious bakery crash and burn, then you'll come begging."

She scoffed.

"Enough."

Clothing rustled, followed by a few grunts as if they were shoving into one another before their heavy footsteps faded. The door slammed, and she sat on the edge of the desk, covering her face with her hands. She counted each shaky breath as she inhaled and exhaled. Begging indeed. Her eyesight would return before she begged Sam for anything.

Of all the nerve, thinking he could come in here and make demands. The bakery was solid. She and Avery made sure of that. The business would see a very high profit at the end of this quarter. More than enough to see them through their slower periods.

She clenched and unclenched her hands at her side. Still, Sam's words had shaken her. Her parents had entrusted her with more than a business. This was their legacy, her heritage, founded by her great-great grandparents. And no matter, what she couldn't lose it.

And not just that, proving to her parents that she could run the business and keep it a success was still a challenge. Even though they'd long accepted she was more than capable, she still felt she had to press her advantage and strive for excellence. *I won't let Sam tarnish the shop as well.*

The door whispered open, then closed. "Are you okay?" Avery's voice was full of concern.

She pressed the heel of her hands against her eyes before standing. "Yeah, yeah. Just peachy." She knew he was close and didn't want to risk running into him, so she held out her hand.

He grasped it and tugged her off-balance.

"Hey."

"You forget that I can see you." His thumb grazed the corner of her eye. "He really isn't worth the tears."

She shoved at his chest, but Avery retained his hold, drawing her closer. He shouldn't be holding her in such an intimate embrace, but goodness, his nearness was just what she needed. She relaxed, resting her head against his chest as he squeezed her a little tighter.

"I just want you to be happy, Penelope. Sam was never the one for you."

With a sigh, she untangled from his arms. "I know that now, and even before. I didn't want to believe he was such an asshole."

Silence stretched between them. What was she going to do now? Just forget about what Sam said and concentrate on work? She lowered her head.

"Are you in some sort of trouble?"

"What? No."

"Then what did he mean about the bakery?"

She shrugged. "At that point, I think he'd say anything to keep me from throwing him out."

"Don't worry about it then, P. The guy is a jerk."

She nodded. Using the desk as a guide, she worked her way around the furniture, and trailed her fingers along the roughness of the wall, until she reached a window. She laid her palm on the beveled glass, the coolness seeping through her skin.

One of her favorite things to do was stand at a window and imagine the view. She'd never seen snow or ice until she moved to Michigan, just before she completely lost her vision. But she adored the wintery stuff. The cold came with its own special beauty. From everything her parents described, it was magic, always indulging her hours of outdoor play.

"What does it look like?"

Soft soled shoes squeaked across the floor, until a warm body met her back. She held her breath as longing whispered through her veins. A hand covered hers, while an arm wrapped around her waist and pulled her close.

"There's frost on the windows." He lifted her hand and dragged her fingers over one corner of the window, a fine glaze of chilliness met her fingertips. "Just outside the window, several icicles hang from the eaves, like glossy sugar cones. Beyond that is a field of white untouched snow, surrounded by a copse of trees.

"The sun is beginning to set, made of brilliant oranges and reds. It's like watching a flame burn across the sky, and when it hits the snow just right, the world shines like diamonds, just like your eyes."

She stiffened against him. *Did he just pay me a compliment?* "Really?"

He turned her in his arms. "You heard me." He grazed her cheek with his knuckle. His voice dropped to a familiar whisper. "I admire you so much."

She knew that voice. How many nights had it riddled her dreams? "Avery?" Pleasure stole through her. She'd worked with Avery for several months now, but he'd always kept their banter light, just friends. When had everything changed? She chewed her lower lip. New Year's Eve. Ever since that moment, he'd taken every opportunity he had to touch her. Her mystery man had been here all along. "It was you."

His thumb caressed her lips, and a tingle thrummed through her entire body. Nipples puckered, while desire moistened her panties. Her breath hitched.

"Yes. I can't resist this any longer." Their breaths briefly mingled before his mouth slanted over hers.

The kiss was unexpected but welcomed. If she had any doubts before, they were now erased. Desire flooded her veins, trickling between her thighs with every flutter of his lips. He held her closer, molding her soft front to his hard frame. How had she missed this before?

Her breasts ached for attention.

She had dreamed of being in his arms, his kisses trailing her skin, for too many nights to count, and now, she found him. She curved her arms around his neck, her fingers drifting over his smooth scalp. But why had he kept his feelings secret?

Abruptly, she pulled away.

He sighed, lowering his head. "Yeah. You're right."

She clutched at his shoulders to keep him from moving. "Right about what?"

"I shouldn't have kissed you." The dejection in his voice tugged at her heart.

She chuckled. "That's not it." She sounded breathless to her own ears, yet... she stepped closer. "In all the time I've known you, I've never taken the time to learn what you look like."

"Please, take your time." He rested his hands at her waist, holding her in place.

Maybe she was still a little muddled from his kiss, but she needed to know.

She drifted her fingertips over his head. Completely bald… well, a few downy patches, as if he'd missed a couple spots. Wide forehead met thick, bushy brows. He had long lashes and deep eyes above a narrow nose and flared nostrils. His ears came next. They sat close to his head and studs pierced his lobes. She lingered there a moment, trying to decipher the stones.

"Diamonds," he answered her unspoken question.

She nodded and moved to his strong jaw which tapered to a rounded cleft chin. He was simply handsome. She cupped his cheek and traced the outline of his lips. Not too thin, not too thick. Rising on tiptoe, she brushed her lips to his.

His hands tightened at her waist.

"No?" She stayed where she was, locking her fingers behind his head.

"Don't tease me, Penelope. I can't handle that right now."

"I'm not the one who started this." She pressed her mouth to his, not giving him or herself an opportunity to say no.

He tasted so good, like chocolate and sin, of decadence and indulgence, of promises better left unspoken. There was so much in his kiss; she wanted to stay right there, in this moment, and take it all in.

He cinched her tighter as his mouth moved over hers, accepting her invitation and issuing one of his own. His erection pressed low against her abdomen.

She wiggled her hips, and he lifted her, bringing her core in full contact with him.

Lightning whipped through her veins, and she clung to his shoulders as he thrust against her. Taking the kiss further would be a simple and easy task, one she could do without hesitation. But she needed to know why he kept his feelings a secret?

Loud knocking reverberated through the room, they broke apart, but Avery did not release her.

"Penelope, are you still in a consult? One of the vendors needs your signature, and I can't find Avery." The voice belonged to one of the cashiers, Becky.

"I'll take care of it," Avery murmured against Penelope's lips. "Be right there, Becky."

Penelope rested her head on his shoulder a moment.

"Oh, okay. Thanks." Footsteps faded.

"Seems as if duty calls." He lowered her to the floor.

"Yeah."

"We'll talk later." He rested his hands on her shoulders, then gently raked his fingers through her hair and smoothed down the front of her shirt. "Now, it doesn't look like you've been making out with your assistant in the consult room."

She giggled while heat touched her cheeks.

He tugged on a lock of her hair. "I love the color you went with this time. A beautiful deep red."

"Thanks."

He pressed her cane into her palm and left.

She touched her lips. *He sure does know how to kiss.*

Chapter Five

Avery Cheatham bustled through the shop, stacking boxes for the last of the forgotten candy order. He centered the boxes on the ledge of the pass-through window. It allowed him to look from the prep area where he was to the main showroom of the bakery. The window even had folding shutters which could be closed and used to display waiting orders. Now, it was just a matter of waiting for someone to pick them up. The other workers were gone for the day, and the shop was now quiet, except for the occasional hum from the equipment.

Stainless steel tables glistened in the low light. A forgotten apron marred the perfection of the room. He retrieved the wayward item and tossed it in one of the laundry bags hanging from a hook in the corner.

One of the things he liked most after a days' work was taking in the quiet after everyone had left. The last of the days' baked goods cooled on the mesh covered racks—that were easily seven feet and held full-size baking sheets. Four of them sat in the farthest corner, near a long wooden butcher block table. A cork board hung above, dotted with cake orders. A plastic box, the size of a shoe box, held the completed orders.

A light flickered, and he made a mental note to switch out the bulb before he left. His eyes shifted as the bulb forced his attention to the dusty shades. He'd schedule a cleaning party for any employee wanting extra hours. Maybe he should have them add a fresh coat of paint too, atop of the cleaning. The industrial white walls were already starting to fade.

Satisfied there was nothing more to be done, he grabbed the clipboard for tomorrow's production. Raised dots ran below the printed words. That was his doing. Every piece of paper that came into the shop, he wanted to be sure Penelope could access it.

He'd worked with Penelope for about seven months now and not once had she noticed him. To her, he was just her seeing eye person, her right hand, her assistant.

But he wanted *more* than that.

He'd wanted to tell her how he felt on New Year's Eve, but after the fiasco with Sam, Avery didn't really see a way to tell her. He wanted to give her the time she needed, but working with her and after their first shared kiss, that had become increasingly difficult. All he wanted was to get her alone and whisper what he wanted to do to her. *And kissing her…*

The kiss in the consult room had been unexpected, but the way she touched him… A sigh left his lips; he wanted to feel her hands on him again. If they hadn't been interrupted, maybe he'd have learned what it was like to feel her fingertips roaming his entire body.

His groin tightened as desire pooled. He was sure of one thing; she was no longer oblivious to him.

A smirk curved his lips. But he needed to be sure she wanted him for *him* and not because she was looking to fill a void in her life. There were still two more days before Valentine's Day, and while he wanted to profess his love for Penelope now, he needed to wait.

A loud crash followed by muffled swearing drew his attention. *Sounds like Penelope knocked something over. But just in case…*

"P?" Avery called out.

"I'm fine," she yelled back.

He strolled through a set of beige swinging doors across a short patch of gray concrete to the back room and stood in her office doorway. The space was neat and tidy. The desk with its computer and another device which held a screen, but he knew to be a scanner that could read documents, waited patiently on the vacant surface. Not even a clutter of pens or paperclips could be seen. There was a framed photo of an older couple embracing a younger Penelope. A grunt dragged his attention to the drab gray concrete.

Several books had toppled to the floor. She was on her hands and knees, her voluptuous derriere tempting as it wiggled in the air as she patted the floor in front of her, moving in a slight circle, gathering the fallen books into a small stacked pile.

When she'd gathered all the books, she cradled them in her arms and pushed to her feet. "Are you done staring?"

The amusement in her voice startled him from his reverie. "No, but I enjoy staring at you."

He leaned against the doorjamb, his gaze drifting over her. She had such beautiful, flawless skin, the color of rich pastry cream or a pale vanilla custard. And her hair was red. Not any red, but a dark ruby. Out of all the hair colors she'd had since he'd known her, this one was his favorite. He longed to plunge his fingers through the silky strands again and plunder her sweet, soft lips.

He straightened. She'd discarded her chef's coat, revealing a low-cut black tank top. The scoop-necked blouse allowed him a generous view of her breasts. Such delight, he longed to hold their soft weight in his palms.

She was lush and curvy, just the way he liked it. No tightly toned arms or abs, just delicious sexiness, poured into a sinfully voluptuous body. He'd lost count of the number of fantasies he already had about her.

"You're staring again."

Avery chuckled. "Your ability to know what I'm doing is uncanny at times."

"We've worked together for a while now." She carefully lowered the books onto her desk. "Why did you kiss me?"

A tiny bing-bong chimed, signaling that someone had entered the shop.

"Hold that thought." He spun on his heel and hurried to the front of the shop. Equal parts of dread and pleasure flowed through him at her question. Kissing hadn't been part of the plan, but seeing the hurt on her face sparked his need to take it away. He wanted her to know why someone would be interested in her.

He smiled at the customer standing at the counter, quickly made change and hefted the box of candies. The least he could do was carry them out. By the time he returned and locked the door, Penelope stood at the cash register, her brows knit together, while a frown tugged at her pouty lips.

"What's wrong?" He was already giving the space a once over. A glance to his left assured him no one lingered in the corridor, though the consult rooms and all the doors were still closed. He scanned the main portion of the bakery. The display case gleamed from a fresh wipe down. Not a single fingerprint marred the surface. The lights inside the case were dark, but it didn't detract from the temptation of cupcakes topped with ganache and decorated with chocolate curls, or the half trays of cookies. A few birthday cakes, their pretty flowers or frosting balloons waiting to be personalized. All in all everything was the way he left it.

"I found an envelope on my chair."

"Oh?"

She placed the stiff white paper on the counter. "It told me to wait right here."

Avery stood on the other side of the divide. "Did it?"

She tilted her head to the side, a curl slipped over her shoulder, just brushing her breasts. "Is there someone else here?"

"We're the only ones here." He covered her hand, drawing tiny circles on her skin with his thumb. *How does she manage to keep her hands so soft?*

"Oh."

"Something wrong?" He studied her, noting the slight inhale, and how her eyes widened at his slight caress. "Your skin is so soft."

She shook her head. "Avery?"

"Hmm?"

"Did you send those gifts?"

"What do you think?"

A smile creased her lips. "Why?"

"I thought it was obvious." He moved from her hand to her wrist. "I like you, not just as my friend, but as something far more intimate, Penelope. You have strength and vibrancy and all I want is a chance to prove that I can be your lifetime Valentine."

She ducked her head, her hair hiding her face. "I don't even like that holiday."

"Yeah, you do. Otherwise, you wouldn't be out here, wanting to know who sent you those gifts."

"You made sure I could read those cards," she said, a catch in her voice.

"Of course."

"Why didn't you say something before?"

"That's what I was going to do New Year's Eve, but things didn't work out as planned."

"Did you know what was going on? I mean… with Sam and Sheila?"

"No." He twined his fingers with hers. "I realize this isn't the ideal situation, but I can't let another day go by without you knowing how I feel about you."

She inclined her head. "You never said."

"I'm saying now."

She was silent.

"P?"

"Every night since New Year's, all I could think about was that moment when my mystery man—you—kissed me. I've been looking for you."

He leaned across the counter. "Well, look no further." He lowered his voice to a whisper. "I'm right here, and I'm not going anywhere."

"You don't have to wait with me, James," Penelope said as they stood in the vestibule of Avery's building. "I'm perfectly capable of standing here by myself."

"Have you ever been here before?"

"No, but—"

"After what Kassie said, I think it's best if I wait with you."

She narrowed her eyes. "What did Kassie say?"

"Sam was making a nuisance of himself."

"Yeah. He's trying to buy the bakery." Footsteps echoed on the tile. "As long as he stays away from me, at the business and at home, I will be fine."

Crisp, woodsy smoke with a hint of chocolate wafted to her nose. "Thank you for bringing her, James.

I'll make sure she gets home." Avery slipped an arm around her waist.

James coughed. "The uh—yes. The missus wanted me to give you this."

Fabric rustled, and the faint chime of metal on metal reached her ears. *What is going on?*

"Oh. Oh."

Even Avery sounded a bit surprised to her ears.

"Tell Mrs. Tilman I said thank you. Penelope's in good hands."

A hand touched her sleeve. "Enjoy your evening, Miss Penelope."

Before she could answer, Avery propelled her forward. Their footsteps sank and were quickly muffled by thick carpeting. "What did he give you?"

"Something for tonight."

"Well, that's helpful."

He chuckled. "Stand here for two seconds."

"If your intention is to blindfold me, I'm already blind."

A faint *ding* and doors whooshed open. Avery ushered her forward. Another click and the floor rumbled upward.

He swung her around and pressed her back to a cool, solid surface. She rested her palms on his chest. The silk of his shirt was smooth beneath her fingertips, and she lingered, relishing the softness of the material. With reluctance she moved on, finding his tie. She longed to explore more but decided she may not have the willpower to stop.

His breath mingled with hers as he moved closer. "You're rather incorrigible too."

She wound his tie around her hand and held him in place. "You started this, remember? All you had to do was tell me the truth while we waltzed on the dance floor. Instead, I've had hot, steamy sex dreams and no relief for an entire six weeks."

Avery swept a feather-light kiss on her lips, teasing and nibbling. "Is that all?"

The elevator lurched to a stop and the doors whispered open. They exited. Not a sound could be heard as they walked a short distance on thick carpet. They stopped. A click sounded to her left, and she was hauled forward. The door to his condo closed behind them. Rosemary and chocolate scented the air. He pressed closer, and the spiciness of his cologne wrapped around her, dragging her attention back to him.

"That's more than enough."

"Imagine how I've felt, watching you every day." He unbuttoned her coat and brushed the garment from her shoulders. "Wanting to hold you close." He trailed a finger along the swell of her breasts, above the low neckline of her dress. "This shade of blue compliments your hair and your skin." His lips followed the same path his finger had.

Shivers of want rippled through her, dampening her panties. "Thank you," she said, desire making her voice breathless.

"Do you trust me, Penelope?"

She lifted a hand and palmed his cheek. "I wouldn't be here if I didn't."

He threaded his fingers through her hair and tilted her head back. "Your kiss has haunted my dreams." He moved her hand and placed it on his erection. "You're not the only one wanting here."

"Ave—" His mouth dropped on hers, demanding all she had to offer. She sank into his kiss, opening for him, sighing when he deepened it. Penelope learned the shape of him through his slacks, but it wasn't enough; she needed no barriers.

With practiced ease, she unbuckled his belt, unhooked his pants, and fumbled with the zipper on his fly.

"Be sure," he murmured against her cheek before trailing kisses along her jaw, to the sensitive hollow of her shoulder.

She answered by plunging her hand down the waistband of his boxers, curling her fingers around his thick, hard shaft. Such a contradiction. Velvet encased iron. There were some fantasies that needed to be lived.

She tore her mouth from his and dropped to her knees, shoving his underwear down as she went. A couple of shimmies later, and his pants were free of his legs. His fingers tightened in her hair when she blew a stream of air across the broad smooth head. She brought the tip to her mouth and curved her tongue around it.

His taste exploded on her tongue, crisp, clean, and all male. An addictive aphrodisiac and she wanted *more*.

A tremor ran through his body as she moved her head back and forth. She gently cupped his sac. Above her, Avery went still.

She continued her slow exploration, licking and sucking. His guttural noises and his fist in her hair spurred her on. She wrapped a hand around his now slippery cock, timing her strokes with each intimate kiss, then drifting the other hand between her thighs, shoving her panties aside. Her fingers delved between her dewy folds, finding her little pearl hard and ready.

She made a noise in the back of her throat as she swallowed him and flicked her fingers over her clit. He held her in place, her nose buried in the fine tangle of pubic hair before he released her and withdrew. Reluctantly, she allowed him to slide from her mouth with a final lick and kiss.

He helped her to stand before claiming her lips. He nibbled from corner to corner, leaving no doubt about his intention this evening. She opened to him, meeting and dueling with his tongue, briefly sucking on it before submitting to his dominance.

"Wrap your arms around my neck, P."

She rushed to comply, allowing her head to fall back as he kissed the slope of her throat. He lifted her, cradling her to his chest and moved forward. A moment later she was settled on a bed. Avery's scent rose around her, and he followed her down.

He swept her dress and bra straps from her shoulders, his mouth warm and moist on her skin as he kissed his way from shoulder to shoulder. For once, she was glad she wore a wraparound dress. Easy on, easy off. And he was taking his own sweet time peeling her clothes off.

She moved to unknot the belt, and he shackled her wrists with his hand.

"My treat. I get to unwrap the goodie," he murmured.

A ripple of anticipation sizzled through her body, tightening her nipples. With his free hand, he untied the belt at her waist. When he jerked on the end, she shifted and felt the material pull free of its loops. She pulled her arms from her dress, and it was removed from her fingers. A moment later, the cloth was wound around her wrists.

She swallowed hard. Her hands were her way of exploring the world around her. If she couldn't touch anything, it didn't quite exist for her.

"Do you trust me?"

He straddled her thighs, the smoothness of his dress shirt tickled her skin while he cupped her breasts, letting his thumbs swipe over her nipples. He'd asked her that before he carried her into his bedroom. She did trust him. Always had.

She allowed the tension to seep from her body and settle into the bedding.

"I do," she finally said.

He leaned forward, his erection brushing her abdomen. His tie skittered over her flesh, only to rest across her lips and nose as he raised her arms above her head. The slip of silk lifted from her face, and he sat back. A moment later, his weight left her completely, and she shivered from the absence of his heat. Wiggling her legs, she drew her knees up and planted her feet on the comforter.

She could feel the weight of his scrutiny as it drifted down her body. She *wondered how she looked to him?* Did he find her curves sexy or wished she were thinner?

She tugged on the restraints.

"What's the matter, Penelope?"

His voice came from her left, and she turned her head in that direction. "N-nothing," she replied

"Liar."

Heat cruised her cheeks.

"Tell me. What's wrong?"

"Do you like what you see?" She held her breath, waiting for the answer, hoping it was what she wanted to hear.

"Immensely."

A frown tugged at the corners of her mouth. Was that enough? Somehow she expected him to elaborate.

He laughed.

"And now you're making fun of me," she said.

"I can show you better than I can tell you."

"Why not do both?"

The mattress dipped beside her. His hand rested on her knee before sliding down her thigh and back again. Everywhere he touched, her skin tingled. She craved more. His fingers skimmed the waistband of her panties, then trailed over the crotch. Desire danced along her damp folds and pulsed within her core. The light stroking continued, and she squirmed.

He hooked his thumbs in the elastic and dragged the triangle of silk over her hips. Cool air raced across her nether lips, intensifying the ache. He reached up and unclasped her bra, baring her breasts.

"Such beauty." He circled one pert nipple with an index finger. "All this lushness." He skimmed his other hand over her curves before cupping her mons. "And it's mine."

She sucked in a breath as he stroked her swollen lips, slick with her desire. Up and down, over and over. She wiggled her hips, seeking relief. When he finally dipped a finger in her moist heat, she wanted to weep.

"After tonight, there's no going back, Penelope. You've been in my heart for so long, I want you in my life and in my bed." He curled his tongue around her nipple while fondling the other.

Tears burned behind her lids at his words. No one had ever spoken anything like that to her before.

He lifted his head. His breath fluttered against her skin. "This isn't some passing infatuation, Penelope." He sucked hard on her tit, and she felt the tug on her throbbing clit. He lavished attention on the other one.

She whimpered from longing, arching her back to push the sensitive orb farther into his mouth. He left her breasts, then proceeded to trail kisses down her torso, over her soft belly where he lingered at her belly button before moving on, feathering his lips over her mound.

Penelope sucked in a breath as he flicked his tongue across her hip, then pressed a kiss to her inner thighs.

She tried to close her legs, but he slipped between her knees, his wide shoulders holding her open.

The warm trailing of his tongue across her heated core shot her hips off the bed. Her world narrowed to the man tempting and teasing her. This was so much better than a dream. He traced her labia with his thumbs before holding them open, exposing the little button of nerves. A gentle lick. The saliva dried in her mouth.

"Are you always this responsive?" He swirled a digit up and down her nether lips, tapping her clit with each pass.

"I don't think I've ever been this turned on," she admitted. Cool air replaced his body heat, and she shivered. Clothing rustled. She shifted on the bed, closing her legs. She squeezed her thighs together, attempting to alleviate the worst of the ache.

"Let's see how hot you burn before you combust, shall we?" He grasped her ankle, skimming a finger along the delicate flesh. She clenched her hands into fists. Delicious shivers raced to all erogenous zones. He dragged a thumb along her instep. His lips followed. Lightning danced through her veins, zigged into her clit, hardening her nipples.

She whimpered as he sucked her big toe, writhing as he lavished attention on each of her tootsies. Her cream trickled, slicking her thighs. He switched to her other foot. All she could do was squirm and moan against the sheets. Pleasure rocked her body with each nip of his teeth and swirl of his tongue until she was a quivering mass of need.

Each touch ratcheted her passion a little higher until she was more than ready for the foreplay to end and to be sent into oblivion. Instead, he worked his way up her legs, leaving butterfly kisses in his wake.

When he finally settled between her thighs, teasing her most intimate flesh with the tender caresses of his tongue and lips, she knew this was reality and he was going to make all her dreams come true.

"Please, Avery."

He chuckled. The sound vibrated through her center, adding to the silvery sensations sliding over and through her. He fastened onto her tiny pearl and sucked. Her breath caught in her throat as her hips moved of their own volition.

Penelope hummed, her cries growing louder. He drove two fingers into her wet heat, filling her but not quite enough. When he added a third, her world exploded. Each rhythmic pulse of her pussy sucked at his fingers, hoping to keep them within the haven of her body.

Avery moved up her body, leaving her quivering flower to trail kisses along her torso instead. He reached her lips, sharing her unique flavor with her. She eagerly accepted his kiss. His arousal pressed to the entrance of her core; she shifted, and the head slipped in.

She moaned into his mouth, yearning for *more*.

He entered her in slow increments, prolonging her pleasure and heightening her arousal. When he was fully seated, she twined her legs with his arching upward. Just that tiny movement nudged her toward another orgasm. He withdrew, almost leaving her body completely, and she felt the loss. When he drove into her again, she felt the merging, not just in her heart but in her *soul* as well.

She greeted each stroke with a thrust of her hips. Anticipation built, lying in wait, ready to strike. He squeezed her breasts as he pounded into her slick heat. He tugged on her nipples, and the world tilted on its axis. She focused on their intimate joining, everything centered on the slide of his cock across oversensitive nerves. The soft sound of flesh on flesh and their combined cries fueled her passion. Her world narrowed, and she slid down the rabbit hole. Her muscles spasmed, gripping the hard cock driving her over the brink.

His guttural moans mingled with her keening cry as his hips slowed, then sped up. He shouted his release. Avery collapsed atop her, resting his forehead into the damp hollow of her shoulder. He reached above, untangling the belt and tie from her wrists.

She wrapped her arms around him, and he rolled her until she sprawled across his chest. Her hair slid over his skin, tickling his sides. He smoothed the silky strands, damp with sweat, away from her face and placed a kiss near her temple.

"I love you so much, Penelope. I'm afraid I'll wake up, and this will all be a dream."

She chuckled. "This can't be a dream. We never get this far." She drifted her fingertips over his chest in restless circles. A damp kiss followed. "I love you too."

Avery closed his eyes, savoring her admission. He tightened his arms around her and squeezed. He'd waited so long to hear those sweet words that he hugged them close as they wound through his heart and settled deep into his soul.

She shifted until she straddled his thighs, his cock stirring beneath her bare bottom. He gripped her waist. "How could I have not known how you felt?"

"I'll forgive you this time," he teased.

A smile creased her lips, and she dropped her head, her hair sliding over her shoulders. "Will you? I may not forgive you for not telling me sooner." As she spoke, she ran her fingers over his body, reawakening his desire. Heat pooled low, and once more, he was hard as a rock.

Her deliberate exploration left him breathless. Where her hands weren't, her lips were, the warmth of her mouth slid along his nerve endings. He hadn't intended to start with dessert, but she was so tantalizing, so…

A groan of satisfaction eased from his lips as she seemed to swallow him whole. Her throat gripped his cock, then he was sliding from the wet haven of her mouth.

He threaded his fingers through her hair, enjoying their newfound intimacy.

Chapter Six

Shrill ringing sliced through the silence.

Penelope bolted upright, reaching for her nightstand but finding nothing but air. She shifted and an arm curved around her waist, pulling her against a lean, hard body. That's right. She wasn't at home.

"Avery, your phone or alarm is going off," she murmured.

She moved again and found herself pinned beneath his body, his mouth covering hers. A moan stuck in the back of her throat as she opened for him. She wound her arms and legs around him, holding him close. Never had any man made her feel so complete, so safe, so cherished as he did. And right now, whatever was ringing could wait.

He abruptly stopped. "Wait. That's the phone." He untangled from her limbs. "Damn. It's too early for work. Shay was opening today."

Penelope sat up as the bed shifted beside her. Something clicked and a momentary flash of light flared before her world darkened again. She dragged the sheet over her breasts, drew her legs to her chest and rested her cheek on her knees.

"What?"

She resisted a giggle. He was just as grumpy as she was in the mornings when someone disturbed her sleep. He was silent for too long, and a finger of dread slipped down her spine. At the gentle touch on her right arm, she twisted her head in that direction.

"The alarm was triggered at the shop again."

She knew who was behind this now. All she had to do was figure a way to catch him. "All right." She kicked off the sheet, scooted to the edge of the bed and stood.

Avery was there before she could truly get her bearings. "I wanted to make you breakfast in bed," he said.

"It's okay." She rested her hands on his chest. "You can do that another morning." She didn't think she'd ever tire of touching him. Slowly, she drifted one hand over his chest until she cupped his cheek. Day old stubble prickled her palm, then she swept her thumb over his lips. A moment later, she rose onto her tiptoes and kissed him. "Let's get to the bakery."

Thirty-three minutes later, they stood in the waiting area of the bakery. The police already completed their inspection, and the newly repaired door was intact. Thankfully, nothing had been disturbed.

"Do you think it was a glitch with the alarm system? Maybe the battery is dying?" She unwound her scarf and unbuttoned her coat.

"I don't think so. Wait here. I'll check things again."

"Are the cops still outside?"

Footsteps scuffed against the floor. "Yeah. They'll probably stay out there until we open." Clothing rustled, and he gripped her shoulders. "You know they're fans of yours. You should give them a cupcake or something."

She laughed. "They'll think I'm flirting again."

"They know you're off limits."

"Interesting. I didn't peg you as the jealous type."

"I'm not." He slanted his mouth over hers. "Stay here while I have another look around. When we walked through earlier, something was bothering me."

"Where am I?"

"If I tell you that, you won't be still." His voice faded as he moved away.

Hinges squeaked. "Something smells weird."

"Stay where you are," came the muffled response.

She smirked. Did he really think that would deter her?

She tilted her head, listening. The hum of the display cases reached her ears. With one hand thrown out in front of her, she carefully walked forward. Something smelled off.

Her fingers touched cold glass and metal, then slipped in something wet and sticky. She wrinkled her nose in disgust. Totally gross. Why hadn't the closing crew wiped down the cases? Someone was getting disciplined over this.

She rubbed her fingers together. The substance was tacky. It wasn't icing or chocolate. Again, she dipped an experimental finger in the goo. There was something familiar about it. As much as she detested the task, she followed the sticky stuff nearly to the end of the counter and stopped. The odor was stronger here. Something familiar. A little sweet, but she couldn't place the scent. She wiped her hand on her coat, then stopped and brought her fingers to her nose, sniffing.

A frown teased her mouth. Lotion? Or maybe … some sort of hand sanitizer? That's what it was. Why would someone squirt that all over the display case?

"Avery," Penelope called. "There's some weird lotion/hand sanitizer on the counter."

Avery stopped mid-stride. He hadn't seen any lotion on the cases when he switched on the lights. He changed directions and headed toward the front again. *Something doesn't feel right.*

"And it feels weird too."

He stifled a groan. What had she walked into this time? Stubborn female. The only time she seemed to follow directions was in bed. Just thinking about what they'd shared most of the night had his cock springing to life. A quick glance at his watch—*yeah, there isn't enough time to indulge in her lush curves before the first employee arrives in thirty minutes.*

Avery rounded a table. The odor hit him then, reminding him of an overheated car and a buffet line. A blur of red hair caught his attention above the swinging doors. *What is she doing now?*

He picked up his pace, some instinct urging him forward.

"There's a small box here. Did you leave another gift?"

Gift? His heart pounded. He hadn't... "No." Through the crack in the swinging gate, he watched her reach for a square-like object nestled between the register and a stack of bakery bags. The paper glistened with a bluish tinge. Warning bells clanged in his head. *That's what is off.* She lifted the lid. "Penelope, no!"

A spark. That's all it took before the entire display burst into flames. Fear and panic culminated in a scream as Penelope stumbled away from the fire, yet the blaze moved with her.

Avery's world narrowed, heart stuttering as he realized the right side of her coat was on fire. Adrenaline shoved him into action. He slammed through the gates, leapt across the counter, and tackled her in one smooth maneuver. He rolled her, snatching her coat from her body and slapping out the remaining flames from her clothes.

"Are you okay?" He ran his hands over her body.

She coughed and moaned but nodded.

Smoke quickly filled the space. Heat singed his face. Pounding and shouting reached his ears.

He twisted his head. The cops from outside crowded the door. With an arm around Penelope, he helped her to her feet and hurried toward the door. No sooner had he twisted the lock, uniforms blurred together as people spilled in, yanking them out.

A coughing spasm wracked his body.

Mr. VIP stood in the middle of the gathered crowd, shivering from the crisp winter air. But the press of bodies surrounding him dampened the worst of the chill. He focused his attention, just like everyone else, on the thick black smoke pouring from the bakery front door.

He ducked his head, forcing his way past two college students for a better look. For one dazzling moment, fire crackled, flaring into a life of its own. In the next instant, it was little more than smoke.

He bit back his disappointment as two blurred figures stumbled out of the building, both hunched over and coughing. He could hear their ragged barks over the traffic noise. He dared to move a step farther, going as close as he could. As the two flickered into focus, he noticed one of them had red hair, while the other was… he muffled a curse. *It's the assistant.* He hadn't counted on him being here to rescue her.

A furtive movement caught Mr. VIP's peripheral. He focused his attention on the man in the tan outer coat. *Ah, Sam, the spurned lover. I wonder what he's doing here? Is he here to gloat as well?* Well, it's not like Mr.

VIP had much to gloat about this time. His little incendiary device hadn't worked as advertised.

With a sigh, he allowed the crowd to shuffle him away from the bakery. *I will just have to try again later.*

Avery glanced around the rapidly filling street. Sirens shrieked their presence as a fire engine rounded the corner, an ambulance not far behind. Smoke billowed from the open door, and Penelope was nowhere to be found.

In the time they'd been pulled from the bakery, they had been separated. The street was now blocked off, making it difficult to find her. Everywhere he looked were curious faces. He drifted his gaze over young and old, hatted and hatless, but not a single redheaded woman among them.

A man with a bowler hat and thick glasses caught his attention. He thought he recognized him, but he turned away before Avery could give it much thought. So he continued his search for Penelope.

With his heart lodged in his throat, he pushed his way through the gathering crowd, shaking anyone off intending to stop him as he searched for the woman he loved. "Penelope!" His voice drowned in the din of shouts and idling engines. "Penelope!" *I have to find her and make sure she's okay.* "Penelope!" *Even to his ears, his voice sounded desperate.*

"Here."

The crowd parted, and there she was: disheveled, shivering, but *alive*.

Relief coursed through his veins and sagged his shoulders. She was seated on the bed of a pickup truck, a blanket wrapped around her body. Her hands, palm side up, rested on her thighs. Soot and tears streaked her face, now reddened from the heat.

He palmed her cheek, leaned down, and kissed her. Without hesitation, she fused her mouth to his, accepting his offer. He pulled away, resting his forehead against hers. "I don't think I've ever been so scared in my life." He smoothed her hair from her face. A few of the strands were singed, but nothing serious.

"Me too." She winced. "I didn't know you could tackle like that."

He chuckled. "Me either. Did I hurt you?"

Carefully, he looked her over, and for the first time, he really noticed her hands. "Oh, my God." He pushed her sleeves up, gently inspecting the reddened flesh. "We've got to get you to a hospital." He glanced around. "There should be some paramedics here somewhere."

Despite the cold air, her hands were swelling and blistering. The right hand was worse than the left, but both appeared raw and painful.

She chuckled. "It burns a little. How bad is the bakery?"

Here she was injured and all she could think about was her bakery. Avery glanced at the building. The fire extinguished before it could do more damage. "We won't be opening today or tomorrow." He cradled her face between his palms. "I'm sorry, P. I know how important this is to you."

"Don't sound so forlorn. Knowing you're safe and the bakery is still standing means more to me than anything else." She sighed. "But my parents are going to flip when they hear about this."

Avery opened his mouth to contradict her and was interrupted by a snide voice.

"Are you ready to sign the bakery over to me?"

A tremor ran through Penelope, and Avery stiffened at the smug voice behind him.

He released Penelope and whirled on his heel. "What business do you have here, Sam?" he demanded. Anger made his voice hard.

Sam shrugged. "I heard all the commotion and wanted to see if Penny had been injured." He glanced at Avery, then to the woman seated on the pickup truck. "You seem to have hurt yourself, and it's a liability to have a blind person in front of an open flame." He grinned.

Had Penelope been by herself, or he'd been too far away to help, Penelope could've hurt more than her hands. And this man was gloating and grinning like he'd won the lottery. Sam didn't care one whit if Penelope was hurt or not. He just wanted her bakery. Temper snapped. Avery balled his fingers and slammed his fist into the leering man's face. Blood gushed over his hand while bone and cartilage crunched in his wake. He stepped back, shaking out his hand as Sam landed on his butt. A gasp rose from the onlookers close enough to witness the exchange.

"Did you just hit him?" Penelope was at his back, shock in her voice.

"Yes."

"That's him. That's the guy. I saw him sneaking around the bakery earlier." An older man, who held the arm of a uniformed officer, pointed at Sam.

"Yep. That's him, all right. Saw him the other day too." This came from someone else.

"You've got that wrong." Sam stood and wiped his nose with the back of his hand. "I want this guy arrested for assault. He broke my nose."

"From where I stood, it looked like you took a face plant," the older man said.

Several others in the gathering crowd nodded in agreement.

The officer approached Sam, handcuffs in hand. His eyes widened and he stepped away. "What are you doing?" he yelled, slapping at the officer.

Avery watched in grim satisfaction as two officers wrestled a screaming, protesting Sam to the ground and cuffed him. A smattering of applause rippled through the crowd.

"Avery, what's going on?" Penelope nudged him.

He turned, dragging the blanket more fully around her shoulders. "Sam is being arrested."

"Oh."

"Yes. And you need medical attention." He propelled her toward an EMT. "I need to know you're okay."

Chapter Seven

"So you guys were right." Penelope carefully rested her bandaged hands in her lap and leaned closer toward the phone. She had both her best friends on speaker.

"Of course we're right," Moira agreed.

"We know scum when we hear it." This was from Violet.

"The authorities here received some pretty convincing evidence of fraud, embezzlement, and a few other crimes. You wouldn't know anything about that, would you?"

Silence but she could hear their smiles.

"Figured as much." She paused, blinking rapidly to contain her tears of gratitude. "Thanks."

"No problem," Violet said.

"So, how bad is the bakery?" Moira asked.

"Seriously? You ask about the bakery, after she tells you she was set on fire?"

"Well, obviously, she's okay. She's talking to us."

"Obviously."

Penelope chuckled. "We should be open for business in a couple of weeks. There was some smoke damage. Until then, we're leasing a place up the street from us. I'm out of commission for a couple of months though. My parents are coming back to help." The last was said with a grimace.

No matter what argument she tried, her parents insisted on flying to Michigan to help out until she returned to work. On some level, she felt like she had failed them. But as Avery had pointed out, the same thing could've happened to him or any of the other employees for that matter.

That information only slightly mollified her. Here, her hands had second- and third-degree burns, she could barely dress herself, and it would be at least two months before she could hold a pastry bag again. If Avery hadn't been there, her injuries would've been much worse.

"And how's Avery?" her two friends chorused.

"He's just fine. Hovering." Footsteps scuffed the floor behind her. Hands settled on her shoulders. "Say hello, ladies."

"Hi, Avery."

"Hello, ladies."

"Thanks for saving our girl," Moira said.

"And putting out her fire."

Heat cruised Penelope's cheeks. "Hanging up now." She reached for her phone. A hand closed over her wrist.

"I've got it," Avery murmured.

"Happy Valentine's Day," the women chorused, then the line disconnected.

"You've got some pretty cool friends there." Avery turned her chair so she faced him.

She nodded. "They are the best at what they do."

"And it is Valentine's Day... a little late after all the excitement."

She tilted her head, a smile teasing her lips. "Not my favorite holiday."

He chuckled. "Too bad, because I got you a few things to celebrate."

A rich, fragrant chocolate scent passed beneath her nose which was then replaced by a lighter sweeter perfume. Her smile widened. Flowers. "Candy and roses?"

"Very perceptive, and there's one more thing." Clothing and paper fluttered, then a faint grunt before he rested his hands on her knees. Hinges creaked.

Penelope lifted her hands and laid them on his arms, slowly sliding them up until she reached his face. Damn. With most of her fingers bandaged, she couldn't tell what was happening. The only fingers waltzing in the wind were pinky and ring finger on her left hand. She used those to stroke his cheek.

"I don't like this, Avery. Not being able to touch things makes me feel helpless. I don't like that."

He kissed her fingertips. "It's just for a little while."

She pouted. "I still don't like it."

"How about this? Be my Valentine?"

She leaned forward until her lips met his. "Of course."

He carefully pressed her palm to his face. "No. I want you as my Valentine for the rest of our days. Marry me?"

"I…" She snapped her mouth closed. "Are you… but…"

"I don't think I've ever seen you so flustered." His fingers touched hers, and a moment later, something cool and metallic slid onto her ring finger. "It's just a little something I've thought about since our first kiss."

Tears burned her eyes. For the second time in her life, she wished for her sight so she could see the beautiful ring he'd slipped on her finger. "Since our first kiss."

He caressed her lips with his thumb. "Yes. Although, nowhere in my visioning did I imagine you being injured. Naked, yes." She giggled. "Injured, no. So what's your answer?"

"I'll forever be your Valentine." Her heart melted as he wrapped his arms around her waist and fastened his mouth to hers.

At last, she'd found her mystery man.

The End

Author Bio

Lynn Chantale, a romance novelist, short story writer, and part-time background singer, has published many stories across several genres. Her works *include Sex, Lies, and Joysticks*, *True Detective Series*, and *Broken Lens,* to name a few.

When she's not actively planning world domination, she's dominating her household, family, and her cat, Shakespeare. You can visit her at any of her cyber haunts:

Website: https://www.thehouseoflynn.com

Twitter: https://twitter.com/lynnchantale

Amazon Author: https://www.amazon.com/author/lynnchantale

Facebook: https://www.facebook.com/LynnChantaleAuthor

Facebook Group Tale's Tells: https://www.facebook.com/groups/talestells

Instagram: https://www.instagram.com/lynn_chantale/

Youtube: https://www.youtube.com/channel/UCHbAParOHDB7cwfSwUtU3cA

More books from 4 Horsemen Publications

Romance

ANN SHEPPHIRD
The War Council

EMILY BUNNEY
All or Nothing
All the Way
All Night Long: Novella
All She Needs
Having it All
All at Once

KT BOND
Back to Life
Back to Love
Back at Last

LYNN CHANTALE
The Baker's Touch
Blind Secrets
Broken Lens
Time Bomb

Blind Fury
VIP's Revenge
Chef's Taste
The Gold Standard

MANDY FATE
Love Me, Goaltender
Captain of My Heart

MIMI FRANCIS
Private Lives
Private Protection
Private Party
Private Desires
Run Away Home
The Professor
Our Two-Week, One-Night Stand
Can't Fight the Feelings

Discover more at 4HorsemenPublications.com

www.ingramcontent.com/pod-product-compliance
Lightning Source LLC
LaVergne TN
LVHW041642060526
838200LV00040B/1681